The Dream Photographer

Andrew Thurlow

Andrew Thurlow

That being said the Dalai Lama is of course real and wonderful.

Carl Jung, Sigmund Freud, Kari Hohne are all real. The quote *"Your vision will become clear only when you can look into your own heart. Who looks outside, dreams; who looks inside, awakes "* comes from letter by Carl Jung, not a published book. It can be found in the collection of his letters, specifically cited as being from Letter Vol. 1, Page 33, and was written in 1916 to a patient named Fanny Bowditch. As a shorter quote well established in the public domain it is included under fair use.

Wally De Bakker is also real but doesn't really play a part, I just love the name.

Ex Australian Prime Minister Bob Hawke, is also mentioned and was also real, but just as a possibility and is not in the book, as such.

Led Zeppelin are real and the living members are mentioned by name but only the song titles are used which are not subject to copyright.

Putin, Xi and Erdogan may resemble current political figures but are really just constructs representing geopolitical antagonists who may be emotionally swayed by a good cup of a regional beverage.

The front and back cover art is created by Andrew Thurlow using the AI at NightCafe https://creator.nightcafe.studio As per the terms and conditions of the Nightcafe platform, the rights to the images are the ownership of Andrew Thurlow as "the creator". See https://creator.nightcafe.studio/faqfor more information.

Big thanks to my daughter Gabrielle for listening, encouraging and helping.

For Mollie, a most beautiful Auntie.

Also by Andrew Thurlow

The Colour of God (2023)

Contents

1. The Volunteer Victim   1

2. The Royal Road to the Unconscious   18

3. Suffering for you, my love   33

4. Trivialities   46

5. Exigency   57

6. Time and the prescription of Cocaine   69

7. The Stimulation of Reptilia Rosea   79

8. Insufficient Dreams   91

9. The Ensuing Struggle   101

10. The Accidental   114

11. Don't ever play Risk without dice   124

12. The future becomes as the past once was   141

Chapter One

The Volunteer Victim

With an enigmatic sigh, Lem pushed firmly against the stark metal handle of his building exit door. The door refused to yield, offering stubborn, silent protest. The morning had commenced, as it usually did, as a debacle, and he hadn't even left the building. Lem's gaunt reflection sneered willfully at him from the sterile glass. He paused for a moment and glared back. He didn't stare to satisfy any notion of vanity, but to check that the core elements of his appearance were in order. He needed to make sure he had no more mishaps.

His morning had begun with a familiar howl from his alarm, which cut decisively through the fragile truce he had made with his thoughts during the night. On this particular day, his eagerness to wake compelled him to reach out more swiftly than usual. Missing the button to silence the alarm, he had knocked over the glass of water by his bed, sending it crashing unceremoniously to the floor. But nothing was going to spoil *this* day. Lem had leapt up to seize the moment, colliding painfully with the frame of his bed, which seemed to be in an obstinate mood. The lump on his shin throbbed as he had hurried through his preparations.

A second attempt at the apartment complex door, saw the stubborn latch surrender its rusty grip, allowing Lem to liberate himself into the world. The walkway light flickered a wave to celebrate his exit, drawing webbed shadows on the paint peeling from the wall. A light rain had formed a chorus line of cheers and caressed the side of his face as the slam of the door thumped its unhappy farewell. Lem had to gather himself, stoically, as he walked toward the station.

'Just breathe,' he sighed. These were the words Mollie would always say, but now they tasted like paste.

Lem had not expected to see the dream photographer so soon. Instead he had assumed he would go on a tedious, lengthy waiting list. He was even more surprised when he received the confirmation out of the blue to attend an appointment the next day. So little time to prepare.

It wasn't like Lem hadn't had a long series of appointments with other people. First, with doctors who sanctimoniously told him to eat more vegetables, less sugar, and lead a balanced lifestyle, or take this pill. Lem couldn't make them understand that it didn't matter what he ate or how much he undertook, vigorous but gentle exercise, the apprehension didn't subside. The psychiatrists seemed to understand better but appeared to have a predilection for the relationship he had with his mother. They wanted to lead it down some sordid sexual path. It was some fixation they had. Maybe too much Freud on the bookshelf. Since Lem was an orphan, how could any of this possibly be connected to his mother?

It surprised Lem little that the public transport journey had been it's usual mix of tedious insanity. He had missed his original tram by the nearest of margins and had to wait patiently for the next. He had spent the time playing with his metal key ring. The half heart was smooth to the touch from years of being rubbed to a fine polish. With the fob in his hand his mind had raced, but his heart had slowed.

After a short wait, Lem had risen quickly and clumsily to greet the arriving tram. As was his way, he had lined up his toes with the flaking iridescent tape marking the road. The hulking carriage seemed to take an eternity to cover the fifty-metre distance it needed to come level. In an apparent warning to his feet, the advertising on the side had screamed 'GAP' at him as the tram slid silently to a stop.

"Open the door," he had barked loudly at the driver, within a second of the tram pulling up. "Some of us have places to be."

The driver returned Lem's request with the same look of contempt he'd come to expect from every tram operator he had ever encountered.

'Did they teach that,' Lem had wondered. Maybe the tram service just attracted men with especially flexible lower eyeball connections.

Lem had taken his seat and waited for the three other passengers to take theirs. He had eyed them impatiently. There was a girl in a hoodie who looked like she had just come home from a night out.

Prostitution.

Drug use.

Electronic dance music.

Maybe she was involved in the black arts, witchcraft, or magic. Lem's mind meandered through options like an elastic band. She wasn't particularly pretty and seemed to have used makeup to detract, creating a tempestuous storm around her eyes.

The second commuter was a student who Lem gave no more than a sideways glance. The student had already taken his seat and looked ready to begin the journey.

Lem reserved the core of his ire for the elderly passenger attempting to manoeuvre an old style shopping cart into the luggage area. Seeing the delay, and needing to get things moving, he had risen abruptly to his feet and grabbed the cart roughly, shouting shakily, "I will do it."

In single swift motion he had hoisted it high above the rail, and plunged the cart down hard into the luggage rack.

The task complete, Lem had turned sharply and called to the driver, "We are all ready!" as he regained his seat.

"Thank you dear," he had heard a whisper from the seat behind him. The smell of lanolin wafted forward from the brown-clad figure.

'How many shades of the same colour can someone wear,' Lem wondered. He raised his hand in a vague, dismissive wave?

The old lady wore a buffeted tan overcoat slightly open to show a coffee-coloured jumper with chocolate stripes. Her chestnut woollen scarf was likely the lanolin culprit. It looked like it was from the nineteen fifties and had made its way to the present through daily use, not locked away in a box or in some fantastic time warp. Lem's gaze had darted wildly from the russet beret to the smoky topaz glasses, finally resting on the smile that accompanied the voice. The gratitude was warm, and her eyes were open and kind.

"We don't all have that much time Mother!" he had exclaimed desperately.

"Sorry dear," she had replied, the corners of her smile straining slightly.

With the passengers intact, the tram had finally pulled away, reaching cruising speed quickly. It was an easy journey, but Lem tensed. He was always uneasy when he was late, and he was always late. Lem returned to the work of rubbing hard on his keychain, hoping the friction would speed up time. When he stopped they had reached Station Blaak, to pick up a single office worker. Lem pondered that it must have been one of those cool, open-plan offices where everyone wore casual clothes and attended team-building sessions more than once a week. Maybe they had a 'Pizza Fridays'. Lem knew very little about office work, it was just his speculation. He didn't spare the new passenger another glance. His cold indifference was a quiet, simmering protest. How dare they interrupt this journey?

His most important journey.

The tram surged forward, rattling at full tilt, as if sensing the urgency in his chest. Just one stop to go. He let out a slow breath and loosened his grip on the fob in his pocket, his finger tips now brushing it with almost reverent care.He might just make it in time. The tram crested the final incline, groaning against the effort. Lem leaned forward, heart pounding, eyes locked on the stop as it came into view. A cage of glass and steel, reflecting what little sun the sky could muster. It was empty. Completely and eerily empty. A chill crept down his spine.

Something must have been wrong.

Returning to the journey, Lem's heart had risen and burst into an endless cascade of glittering fireworks. Thanks to the empty stop he was now pretty sure he was going to make it. To show his supreme confidence he had even taken his hands out of his pockets and gripped the shimmering silver bar of the seat in front of him. Without meaning to, Lem had let out a huge gleaming smile.

If anyone was watching, he was fairly certain they wouldn't understand, or possibly wouldn't even see it as a happy smile.

But it was a very happy event, right up to the moment the tram bell let out its doleful chime.

Lem had almost torn a neck muscle as his head whipped around to see the brown-clad pensioner release the signal button. The aura of her speckled wrists soaked in the tram light like ripened bananas giving a wave, before the sandy glove and the tan coat closed the gap returning them to darkness.

"You need to get off the tram right now mother," he had exclaimed!

She had looked at him with her kind, wide eyes and replied in a soothing voice.

"Yes dear, this market has a special on shampoo. It's the only way what money I have can stretch."

Lem felt he had been left with little choice, so he leapt to his feet and slipped in front of her before she could fill the aisle.

"I will get your trolley," he had shouted over his shoulder.

"It's OK," her words had trailed off in Lem's ears. He really needed a quick turnaround, not a fumbling few minutes of eternity.

The extraction hadn't been an F1 stop, but he had the trolley out on the footpath before the pensioner even reached the exit. Grabbing her elbow to give assistance,which she gladly took, he deposited her beside her waiting trolley in record time.

She turned to thank him, but he was already gone.

Lem received another dull glance from the driver, who nodded casually, alluding to the fact that Lem was a good citizen for helping the elderly.

'Whatever helps you sleep' he thought. 'Just get this metal beast moving.'

He had slipped his hands back into his coat and rubbed furiously at his metal fob.

'Now,' he had thought gleefully, 'the next one is my stop'.

The tram had halted, annoyingly, at a red light, waiting for two cyclists to cross first. Lem was at fever pitch. He had risen to his feet, ready to scream, but instead stood tapping his foot against the rubber lining of the tram's top step.

He pressed the button.

Then again, just to be sure.

He glanced nervously up at the driver, searching for any sign of recognition that he wanted to get off.

Without any fanfare, the tram had pulled up at his stop. The large doors of steel and glass parted, revealing Lem to the world as he hurriedly stepped down and moved on his way. To confirm just how badly late he was, Lem had pulled his phone from his jacket pocket. The lip of the pocket had worn through due to so many time checks. It was four minutes past nine. The silly old woman had added another minute to his already late schedule.

The bakery was only two minutes from the stop but he had decided the only way to make up time was to run. Lem had never been a good runner. Sport, in general, was never his forte. When he was a kid others took to football, hockey, squash, or tennis, but Lem had trouble with his eyesight over distance, and his knees suffered from severe synchronisation issues. The smooth, methodical mechanism of running had always remained a never-ending mystery to him.

But in that desperate moment, it seemed the only option.

"Damn that brown lump to an eternity in black," he had muttered under his breath as he set off.

The streets were empty in that section of Rotterdam, so he had a clear run for a short while before the fog from his mouth came puffing out with the thickness of a French chowder. After about sixty metres, he had slowed to a walk, taken a series of deep, strained breaths, and waited while the air warmed enough for his lungs to settle. Up ahead, so tantalisingly close, he could see the light outside the bakery where they had agreed to meet. Lem took one last breath and braced himself for the cold pain in his chest before he set off on that final definitive run.

Finally at the door, Lem had snatched out his phone.

Six minutes late.

His face had flushed with embarrassment as the taunts of his childhood echoed in his head.

'Late again Lem'.

He had taken another breath, slipped the phone back into his worn pocket, and pushed forcefully on the bakery door.

Locked!

'What the...'

Lem's shoulders slumped in defeat. How could the bakery possibly be closed? Why would anyone set up a meeting at a place that wasn't open?

Still recovering from the small but energetic run, he had pulled out his phone again to double-check the time. He was late, but it was correct. Frustrated he had returned his phone to his pocket. Maybe he got the address wrong? Lem had reached in to pull out his phone again but in his haste, he had torn more of the lining from around his jacket pocket. The phone tumbled to the pavement and lay lifeless. Lem chastised himself and quickly picked it up.

The phone had begun to vibrate, and the Nokia logo had quickly come onto the screen.

"Oh No!" he cried out. The seconds rushed by vexatiously while the phone went through its boot procedure.

Ten seconds.

'It must be broken' Lem had thought. Twenty seconds more passed, but all that stared back at Lem from the black screen was his own frustrated reflection, clouded by finger prints.

"Now, what else can go wrong today?" he had muttered to himself.

Lem stuffed his phone back in his pocket and turned back to the bakery. There were no "Back in Five" signs, no opening hours, and no lights he could see on the inside. Just a solitary outdoor L.E.D globe above the sign 'The Dream Bakery'. When he had first heard the name, he thought it was a great place to meet. He saw it as a sign his troubles were over.

Lem had struggled with his dreams since he was a kid. He would wake up in the middle of the night crying, screaming, and shouting. He moved, and kicked, and walked, wandering into things in the night. He was never going to be an Olympian, but if Lem was honest, he wasn't slightly close to being coordinated, even when he was awake. He could never master physical things. His lack of physical activity during the day had probably been what had kept him so active at night.

As a boy, Lem had grown up in a small apartment in Rotterdam with his aunt, Mollie. She had always worked hard to put food on the table and to make ends meet. As a small child, when living a life of less, Lem hadn't realised what he was missing. He felt he had everything he needed. Lem had never known his parents. Mollie once told him they'd died when he was very young, and the way her face changed made it clear, this wasn't something to ask about. He quickly learned not to press for details.

Still, he remembered believing his childhood was perfect. There were lazy afternoons in the park with fries dipped in mayonnaise, and storybooks read aloud in soft, warm tones. They'd play dress-up in mismatched costumes, and toys seemed to appear like treasures, waiting for him around every corner.

Mollie seemed to know his habits and movements so well. She would often catch him sleep walking and lead him back to bed, making sure he didn't bump into anything. She would wake him up from his sleep, making him feel less detached in those strange moments. She calmed his fears when he was anxious, and amused him when he was lonely or scared. She pre-empted some of his worst dreams, waking him from them and soothing him gently when he was agitated. He never really understood how she did it. Later, he wondered if she'd been watching his dreams instead of just waking him from them. Still, for the first six years of his life, he lived in a kind of cotton-wool world where he was soft, safe, and sheltered.

But school was a different story.

It was there, he first saw what other kids had, and what he didn't. He quickly found his place at the bottom of the pecking order. Always tired, easily distracted, and clumsy, he was unwanted by everyone, and late to everything. When puberty hit, it was less a rite of passage and more a drawn-out ordeal. Not in the usual way, there were no crushes or relationships to complicate things. No one showed the slightest interest.

The worst part was the dreams, which spilled unwanted into his waking life, blurring the edges of reality, until he couldn't always tell whether he was dreaming or awake. Through it all, Mollie was there. In her quiet beauty, she looked after him. She was his rock, his safety, his distraction, and his compass.

Later, after puberty, she began to annoy him, well, truth was everything began to annoy him. She seemed to know everything he was going to do before he did.

How did she know him so well?

He would try hard to do things at the last minute, spur of the moment, to catch her by surprise. But there she was, waiting for him, knowing him, caring for him, calming him. It was infuriating!

Mollie was small in stature, and hardly spoke any Dutch, preferring English with a clear American accent. She had never married and, to Lem's knowledge, never had a boyfriend. She had one job, as an editor, which she did from a small desk in her bedroom. Unless he was with her, she left the house just twice a day to get groceries or run errands and once a week to go to church. To a lost, strange, mixed-up kid, which Lem had most definitely been, she had been amazing. But as he grew into a young adult, she became constricting and irritating.

Lem wanted to make mistakes of his own.

He wanted to listen to Rock and Roll music. He wanted to drive and take drugs. After all, this was Holland. But Mollie would find ways to hold him back, distracting him with other fun things to do. They had cinema visits, board games to play, and books to read. He loved to do those things too, but they weren't the bad things. It was so annoying, but hard to argue with.

Adolescence slipped, almost unnoticed, into adulthood. With time, Lem managed to carve out a fragile peace, an uneasy truce with the life the universe had handed him. There was joy, but there was mostly rhythm. A quiet gratitude. A sense that maybe, just maybe, things could hold. He and his aunt lived that way for years. A life of soft repetition, steady and familiar, until recently on a bitterly cold morning that had shattered it all.

On that day, Lem had woken with a jolt, seized by a fever so fierce it felt like fire in his veins. The memory simmered. He'd been dreaming again, always the same street, scorched by an unrelenting sun, with the air thick and heavy. He wandered its length, calling out, disoriented, desperate. No one came. No one ever did. The pavement beneath him had buckled and turned to quicksand. It sucked him down slowly, cruelly, until he was trapped, limbs heavy, lungs screaming, his body sinking, and melting into the street like wax left too long in the heat.

He could still taste it. A bitter, chemical burn at the back of his throat. And then, he was awake.

Gasping.

Soaked in sweat with the room spinning.

Yet again Lem's bed was a battlefield as he defended his sensibilities against the demons in his head.

But on that morning something had changed. Something had broken loose.

As he would often do, Lem had turned to drink from the glass of water Mollie always left for him on his nightstand. But there was nothing.

'Where was Mollie?' he had asked himself. When dreams got that bad, she was usually there at his side when he woke up.

Lem had gotten out of bed and headed for the kitchen. All the lights were off, and the apartment was cold and quiet. Turning on the kitchen light, he took a glass from the cupboard above the sink. He filled it and drained it quickly, to quench the fire in his mouth. The taste of sand was replaced by the freezing cold water. He hadn't noticed before, but he now began to feel just how cold the apartment was.

'Why was Mollie not awake?' he pondered.

She was usually up well before him, prepared coffee and breakfast, and had already warmed the apartment. He had moved through the lounge toward her room and found the door open. Mollie was dressed in her loose house dress. She lay slumped on the floor, lifeless, like a marionette with her strings cut. Her quiet form sprawled in an unnaturally limp position. Lem really hadn't been able to process the situation well.

"Are you cold Mollie," he had said to her quietly? "You should have more clothes on."

He recalled how icy her body had felt as he touched her shoulder gently. Not sure what to do, Lem had cradled her tiny form and lifted her tenderly, sliding her head onto the pillow and lightly brushing her grey hair to the side to show her peaceful face. Lem had then gripped her ankles gently and guided her legs up to lie her straight in bed. He had slowly drawn the covers up around her chin and tucked in the sides, just like she used to do for him, to make sure he wouldn't fall out of bed if his dreams got wild. At that time, unsure what had just happened, he had drifted back a step in a double take and had almost fallen.

"Mollie."

"Auntie."

Was it the cold? Lem couldn't feel his feet. They had fused to the floor, like a street sign dipped in concrete, covered in tar. He was numb as his world lay withered and cold in front of him. He had waited on the spot for an eternity to wake from the dream, but it was very real.

The painful memory was given a jolt back to reality by the screen of Lem's Nokia, which finally sprang to life, cascading a bright white glow across his face. The cold distracted Lem, and the light rain wasn't helping. The phone had trumpeted its start-up call, and Lem could finally access his email app.

"The Dream Bakery had most certainly been the name of the place."

"What the…"

His mind had raced over possibilities. Was there another Dream Bakery? Was someone having fun with him? No stranger to practical jokes, maybe Lem had been the subject of one, again. He had looked around at the facade.

The Dream Bakery was very plain. A large imposing door of black wood and glass held a vigil in the center, guarded either side by imposing mirrored windows. There was no writing on the glass. All in all, it looked a little boring for a bakery, which was usually a place of light and warmth.

Lem had been hoping for coffee, having missed his this morning on account of his lateness. It was cold, and his brain tended to work slower in lower temperatures, the exertion of the run having long since worn off. He had scanned further around the building and noticed a black dome CCTV camera. Figuring it was trained on him, he had stared at it, straining his neck to make it obvious the camera had his attention.

"The tram was late," he pleaded with the camera.

"Too many old people on public transport, always messing with the schedules," he lied.

Lem wasn't sure the camera was listening.

Maybe the comments were for his own reassurance.

He had looked again and continued.

"I wanted to be early," he said, his voice thin and uncertain.

"It's quite cold out here."

He couldn't tell if the camera was still watching him. Talking to it felt like dealing with shop assistants. They were always avoiding his gaze, offering minimal engagement, yet carrying out the exchange all the same. Women assistants seemed to have perfected the art of looking past him, eyes drifting away, expression flat, their interest reserved for the transaction alone, as if he were just an unfortunate footnote in it.

Lem shifted his weight onto the ball of his left foot, subtly turning away from the camera and back toward the door.

Once again, he felt like a fool, a feeling all too familiar. But this time, he was a fool standing in the rain, talking to a camera. He pivoted on his right foot, prepared to walk away, when he heard the distinct click of a lock disengaging. He placed his wet palm on the cold glass to make sure, and when the door gave under his touch, he pushed through it with a kind of hopeful relief.

***

Joost was not a normal candidate for the priesthood. If there indeed, was such a thing. He had spent years travelling the world, through Southern Africa, then Asia, before moving to South America and finally joining the merchant navy as a seaman. His journey had taken him far and wide where he met a lot of people from a lot of cultures. Joost had always been a happy, friendly loner, moving on, but never maintaining close contact with those he met.

In the late seventies, on a particularly long shore leave in his home port of Rotterdam, Joost had a life-changing push-bike accident. The accident was probably the result of a particularly long session with some very, very good weed. In those days Joost had often self medicated, drugs being the great crutch of the unrequited.

After the accident he was taken to the local hospital, which patched his body, but during his recovery, he found his soul also quite broken. Attempting its repair he had stumbled on God. Or rather, God had descended on him, on the grounds of the park on Grotekerkplein. The park was attached to the church and on a cold day he had seen the light on and taken a walk inside. He must have looked a poor sight, his arm in a caliper and bandages covering a significant

12

part of his torso. But with a new joy in his heart, he had walked up to the priest, who was placing out Bibles amongst the pews, and told him straight.

"I would like to be a priest and talk to God."

The priest, Gert, was a kindly old man who had sat Joost down, provided him with a cup of tea, and waited patiently for several hours while Joost unravelled his story. Gert was very sympathetic and a good listener, and after hearing him out, told Joost he should come back tomorrow and see if he still felt the same.

Joost returned the next day, received a similar cup, had a similar conversation, followed by a similar proposition. He returned the following day, and the day after that.

After a week and many difficult, personal conversations, Gert told him there was no room for him in the priesthood. That Joost's faith simply wasn't strong enough. Joost returned every day for another week, then another, often just sitting alone in the church. At the end of the month, Gert told him again that there was no room in the church for him and that his faith was simply not strong enough.

Joost didn't know what that meant, and Gert wouldn't tell him. So, to show strong faith, he continued to return.

Whether this was mistaking attendance for faith or not, finally a sign was sent.

Gert had passed quietly in his sleep of natural causes, and it seemed the church had no replacement. Religion in Holland was on the decline, and the visiting bishop was most interested in talking to Joost.

The bishop was very well meaning and helped him enter the priesthood. After his studies and with a few years working under other priests, either by fate or due to the aforementioned decline, Joost was assigned back to Rotterdam.

Joost's memory of Mollie's passing surfaced a little later in the day than Lem's had.

He'd run into Lem in the park. It wasn't strange to see him there, but seeing him without Mollie was unusual. Joost had always approached Lem with caution. He had a reputation for bad tempers and sudden mood swings. Joost had previously been on the receiving end of both. Sometimes, Lem didn't respond at all. He cleared his throat and steeled his resolve as he approached.

"Everything all good," Joost asked?

Lem looked up from the cold grey park bench. He said nothing, but his eyes told a painful story. He had sighed and taken a large mouthful from the polystyrene cup he was holding.

"How is your Aunt Mollie." Joost asked, more cautiously?

"She's dead." Lem replied, bluntly.

His hollow eyes absorbed the dull grey from the morning cloud's filtered light.

Joost sat gently on the cold park bench next to Lem.

"When did this happen?"

"Today." Lem's shoulders dropped, crestfallen. His face fell, locking into an intense staring competition with the rotting leaves on the damp ground.

"Oh, Lem, I'm so sorry for your loss. I saw her just yesterday in the market." Joost consoled. "How did this happen?"

Lem was in no mood.

"I don't know." he said, his focus shifting.

Joost looked at him with a mix of surprise and concern.

"What happened? Did she go to the hospital?"

Time passed with a punctuated pause.

"No. Still at home."

"At home? Did you let someone know she was unwell?"

"No." Lem exhaled the reply with a cutting resignation.

"So, you must." Joost said. "We must let the authorities know she is unwell."

Lem shifted uneasily.

"Too late."

"I'll come with you, to check on her," Joost said getting more insistent.

Mollie would never confirm to Joost that Lem had any behavioural problems, but Joost knew he was not capable of handling such complex situations. Who ever heard of a grown man still living with his aunt.

Lem shifted again, uncomfortable, but Joost persisted.

"Let me help you my friend."

They weren't friends, but Joost knew Lem wouldn't accept help from a stranger, and the two knew each other well enough.

"Okay." Lem replied breathing through his teeth.

The trip to the apartment was taken in silence.

Lem trudged unwaveringly, while Joost followed quietly.

Joost had never been to Mollie's apartment. The two had only met as part of church working groups or around the marketplace. He was surprised Mollie had such a small apartment but not surprised that it was so impeccably kept. She had always struck him as a very accordant individual.

Lem hovered uneasily at the entryway and pointed Joost toward Mollie's room. Joost found the light switch and illuminated the room, then moved resolutely to the bed. He looked over his shoulder before easing back the bed cover.

Mollie's face was grey but peaceful. She looked so much thinner than she had the day before, and even though his time in the church had brought him into contact with many dead bodies, he was still shocked by the change in such a short time. He reached for her hand and checked for a pulse.

Nothing. She was cold to the touch.

He replaced the bed cover and turned to Lem who was waiting expectantly in the doorway.

"Sorry, Lem." Joost said sympathetically. "She is at peace now."

Lem went to turn and leave, but Joost preempted him.

"Lem," Joost asked.

"What happened?"

"I don't know." said Lem.

"She didn't bring my coffee." He added, looking truly sad. "Then I found her cold on the floor. I put her in bed to warm her up, and I went out to get coffee from the Café in the square."

Joost was a bit taken aback by the recount, but he knew enough to know that was just Lem's way.

"Did you call anyone?" Joost asked.

"No," replied Lem.

"We must call the police, they'll come to remove her."

The police had never bothered Lem. He had no experience with them and had never needed to call on them before.

"OK," he shrugged.

Joost was never good at physical contact. But most people accepted a kindly pat on the shoulder or having their hand held by a priest. Lem was not most people. Joost waited for his moment and cautiously placed his hand on Lem's shoulder as the ambulance officers took Mollie's body away. He sat patiently with Lem while the police took his statement. He made tea and tried to be helpful. He didn't believe Lem was a bad guy, and certainly didn't think Lem had done anything untoward.

The day passed slowly, but Joost had learnt to be patient with the progression of both life and death. He tried to pass that patience on to Lem, who clearly just wanted this all to be over.

To his credit, Lem only had one outburst, and it was minor. When the police officer asked if he had hurt Mollie, Lem snapped.

"No! Never!" he replied grimly.

Joost stood up in his defence, and the officer backed off. It was clear there was a deep bond between Mollie and Lem, Aunt and nephew, friends, and more. The officer let it go, and after tidying up some paperwork, exited the house.

Joost made more tea and sat with Lem a little longer. He checked to see if there were enough supplies in the house, and by his count, everything was there for Lem to cook, snack, or get by.

He asked Lem if he would be okay and if he needed anything.

Lem gave no answer.

Joost wanted to call someone, but it was clear Lem had no one else, so he stayed a little longer.

After a full day by Lem's side, Joost decided it was time to make his exit.

He left Lem sitting forlornly at the dining table, seemingly lost in thought. Joost resolved to visit him again tomorrow and reluctantly took his leave.

Chapter Two

The Royal Road to the Unconscious

The hotel had a cavernous foyer, wide and spacious, adorned with lavish decor.

It was built in the nineteen twenties, when everything was worth celebrating. That was just before the crash, shortly after the war to end all wars, but before the bigger war that was inevitably to follow. On the left of the foyer stretched a classical reception desk, replete with a walnut-grain bench, leather side cuffs, brass footrests, and inlaid marble. Clusters of green leather armchairs, plush and inviting, were arranged in threes and fours across the open floor. To celebrate further the ceiling was intricately decorated with swirls and coronets, smiling hand-painted cherubs floating among the clouds and flowers in a dreamy scene of tranquillity. Small brass fans punctuated the opulent ceiling at even intervals with the entire grandeur ringed by an endless cascade of ornate cornices.

On the right, a huge bar area dominated. At the end, furthest from the door stood a majestic staircase rising to the mezzanine from the left and right, extending open arms to embrace arriving guests.

Even though it was huge, the reception desk was empty. The equally spaced small green shades of the brass bankers lamps acted like beacons for where the receptionists should be. It was a reminder of an era before retractable people barriers to shepherd the oncoming masses into a single overworked service agent.

I looked around. The whole place was empty.

A slow dread stirred in my gut and rose like smoke through my chest.

I moved towards the nearest lamp and tapped on the bell that sat warming itself in the lamp's glow.

Silence.

Then, out of the corner of my eye, something shifted near the mezzanine level. I turned and spotted someone in one of the gest bedroom windows. He looked at me unceremoniously, and I returned the favour.

He was about my size, but muscled far beyond my proportions. At first glance, it looked like something had eaten away at his arms, but as my eyes adjusted, I saw they were thoroughly inked. It was hard to make out details from that distance, but the tattoos blanketed both arms. There appeared to be no visible design, no purpose, no class or style, just chaos rendered in ink.

His lips were moving, but no sound reached me. The hotel foyer remained eerily quiet as he mouthed something in big, rounded words, but I couldn't make them out.

He was a strange-looking man, with a small tuft of hair atop his otherwise bald head and an equally small, tufted beard on his chin. As if you could flip his head upside down and nothing would be out of place. Symmetrical in the oddest way.

A cough came from behind me, and the receptionist greeted me curtly.

"Good evening, sir. Welcome to the Hotel Sempiternal. May I help?"

"Interesting guest," I replied, tilting a finger, but not my gaze, toward the upper bedrooms.

"It can be interesting what some people become," she said. "But it takes some time."

I gave her a casual glance. Thick, curly blonde hair tyrannised her features. It wasn't well cut, possibly a wig. The ringlets didn't cascade so much as encircle her head like razor wire on a Stalag perimeter. Her eyes were a cold Nordic blue, offering an icy stare. She had used too much rouge, perhaps to distract from her bulbous nose. None of it quite fit, but it didn't matter.

"I was hoping to check in," I blurted.

"As everybody does, sir," she replied, knowingly, and presented me with a key.

"Welcome back."

Before I could respond, she dropped the key on the desk and turned away, evaporating into a back room.

I had never been here before.

The key was a Moebius loop. It had no room number. I might have missed it, but I didn't recall the receptionist mentioning one either. I struck the bell with three sharp taps, hoping to summon her again.

Time dragged. Eventually, I tapped the bell once more.

I turned, searching for anyone, any sign of life, but the foyer was empty.

I glanced back up at the window. The tattooed man was gone.

Nothing stirred.

Feeling a little dispirited, I drifted toward the bar, hoping for company.

Light bounced off the foyer walls as shadows flickered along the ornate ceiling, the painted cherubs smiling not at me but across the room in their fixed, unnerving serenity. The false movement in the ceiling's shifting light gave the illusion of life, but the place was hollow.

The bar curled deeper to the right, out of sight from the reception and away from the twin staircases. It was cleverly designed, buried deep enough that no sound would reach the sleeping guests above.

It matched the style of the foyer, high wooden shelves stocked with dusty bottles. A dim backlight blurred the labels, familiar brands made unfamiliar by shadow.

The bartender was small, with a pencil moustache and an emaciated frame swallowed by a red velvet waistcoat. He greeted me with a nod.

"Whisky, neat," I said. My usual.

He reached for the top shelf and poured in a single, fluid motion, no excess, no hesitation. I drank it quickly, and without a word, he poured another.

He didn't speak, didn't ask for a room number. No tab. No questions. No other guests.

I drank more as habit took over. I got drunk and, as I often did, fell asleep in the bar. When I woke, there was food in front of me. I ate quickly, hoping it might chase the thumping in my head. Replenished, I set off to find my room. As I passed reception, I rang the bell again to try and get the receptionist's attention, without response.

I followed my instinct and went upstairs.

I passed the window where the man had been earlier and looked in. He was in the room, having sex with a woman on the bed. I watched for a while. They didn't see me. I wasn't aroused and after some time, I moved on. I was still unsure which room was mine as none had numbers, just the same Moebius loop etched on every door. I picked one a comfortable distance from the noisy couple.

Who wants that going on all night?

It was empty. I entered, showered, and put my original clothes back on.

Days passed. At least they felt like they were days.

I drank a lot at the bar. I never ordered, drinks just kept being served, and food showed up when it was time to eat. There was never anyone else around, so I did whatever I felt like. Sometimes, if I drank too much, I just vomited right there in the bar. The bartender never flinched. When I returned later, everything was spotless. Reset perfectly.

As if nothing had happened.

My frustration turned into erratic behaviour. I broke some furniture. I found a chess set and played against myself. One night, in anger, I pissed on it. When I came back, it was all pristine again. The same board, the same pieces, neatly arranged.

Unmoved.

Unmoved like the rest of this place.

Eventually, I wandered further into the hotel. Past the empty hallways and blank doors, I discovered a strange annex. A massage parlour, barbershop, and tattoo studio combined into one. There was also a gym. The parlour was run by a small girl with oversized round glasses. She didn't say much.

Time became meaningless, but by the state of me, a year must have passed. My hair had begun to fall out, and I had no razor. I was unkempt, with a thick, fluffy beard hanging from my face. I hadn't checked in with luggage, and I was still wearing the same clothes I had on when I arrived.

Days slid into each other. I passed the time working out in the gym, playing chess, sometimes with the bartender, sometimes alone, getting tattooed, and having sex with the girl in the glasses.

I didn't try to stop any of it. The monotony washed over me, warm and numbing.

The drink was good.

The sex was good.

The chess was average.

Weeks became months, or longer. Who knew? There were no clocks. No days of the week. Just rhythms.

Habits.

Then one day, as I walked into my room, I heard the bell at reception ring.

Clear and deliberate.

I rushed to the window and looked down. A man was standing there, my size, no luggage, looking slightly confused.

Just like I had.

I cried out, "Get out! Get out!"

But the words went nowhere. Swallowed by the silence.

When I woke, I felt so tired.

Like I had lived a lifetime.

***

Eugene had heard the stories before, each with equal parts of incredulity and clarity. They were always delivered with passion, as if the incident had truly occurred, and as if the dreamer were a poet recounting a tale passed down from an actuary. He had grown tired of the over-exaggeration, the emotional overflow, the convenient exoneration for otherwise intolerable behaviour. Perhaps he had heard it all. Eugene had been interested in dreams for as long as he could remember. He knew dreams could come thick and fast everynight yet few were remembered. Fewer still were shared, and almost none were seriously investigated. He suspected something larger was at play, something that deserved proper study.

His early experiments on himself had yielded unexpected insights. Now he was focused on refining his methods, perfecting his approach before even considering presenting his findings to the world.

He didn't need more tales of hotel-room sex and drunken debauchery.

Whatever truth lay inside such dreams was usually buried beneath boastful embellishment, inflated by the ego of the teller, probably in some desperate way to impress the listener. In his experience, most people dismissed dreams as useless, random sparks of neural static. But Eugene was a Darwinist at heart. If dreams existed, they must serve a purpose. Evolution didn't favour waste. What fascinated him wasn't just the content of dreams, but the how.

How could one hear sound without ears?

See images without eyes?

Feel terror or love without a body to process it?

If dreams were evolutionary leftovers, why did they seem so sophisticated. So deeply human? Was there something more? Had we just scratched the surface?

Dreams had been a relatively unexplored field, which, to most people, held only mystery. In many cases, people would have rather not discussed their dreams. If a dream escaped into the light, someone might have thought the teller mad, deviant, boring, or divine. Dreams of God complexes had not been uncommon, but they hadn't made anyone divine.

Eugene hadn't been a psychiatrist, but he had read a lot. He had read extensively on dream lore and on dream theories, and overall he had thought he understood what was known. Personally, he had felt that it wasn't much, and more research had been needed. Given that the average human spent six years of life dreaming in REM sleep, there should have been lots of data on what they dreamed, what it did to their bodies, and a myriad of statistics and anecdotes. But there had seemed to exist only shreds with very little baseline, very small amounts of stimuli, and when they had been used, most had been drug-based. Even normal dreams had caused people to break their natural sleep position, shouting, talking, walking, and moving as if they were truly awake. REM sleep had also been found in other mammals and birds, so there must have been a history and a reason for dreams.

So Eugene had set about discovering this new Royal Road.

Why had his brain taken things he had seen, things he hadn't seen, things he might have seen, and things he hadn't wanted to see, mashed them together, and presented them in the strangest scenarios, complete with a bag full of emotions every night, multiple times? If it had been a warning, then it had become a little bit of *'boy who cried wolf'* overkill. Most dreams were simple reflections, wants, needs, and desires. This had been where Eugene excelled. He had become a master at the manipulation of thousands of millions of results and the processing of those results by smart helper apps to pinpoint anomalies.

His early results in dream recognition had been inconsistent, but Eugene had persisted. A small modification to his EEG equipment to focus on the posterior cortical hot zone, Dream Central, had marked a key milestone. This had been closely followed by the early development of Eugene's AI. The intelligence hadn't been so artificial. It had been the culmination of Eugene's understanding and the steady growth of lightning-fast rule sets and Large Language Models. This had given rise to D.A.A.I.S.I., the Dream Assisted Artificial Intelligence System Interaction, pronounced *'Daisy'*. Daaisi had interpreted the information and given focus to the key elements of the dreaming individual. It had started out simple, but Eugene had quickly adapted Daaisi to learn from what was interpreted.

His early experiments had been a building experience, but he had been very methodical. Those early electronic recordings had been matched by colloquial recounts of dream memories. Daaisi would process the telemetry, audio and visual results, and pattern match known elements. EEG data from a dream recounted with a red door had shown certain brain activity. A big red door had yielded more refined activity, a small red door had triggered less activity in the same area. The recounted dreams could have been discrepant, but there had been enough positives to give Eugene hope that he had been on the right track.

Eugene, or Daaisi, had begun to recount key elements of his dreams.

"Large fir trees. Forest. Mountains. Large spiders. Hair. Black. No legs. Scream. Silence."

The early results had been clumsy, he had indeed dreamt of spiders. Large black, hairy-legged spiders had attacked him in a forest surrounded by mountains. He had been stuck in the mud and couldn't move. He had been trapped and had tried to scream, but could only manage a mute cry before the dream had ended. He had recalled more detail, and using Daaisi, he would match this recalled information to the brain activity, looking for it in subsequent dreams. Eugene had found it easy to baseline simple forms and colours. The building of objects in Daaisi's database had been based on the dreamer's experience. The more he had been able to focus on himself, the more Daaisi would learn and recount.

Weeks and months had passed as he built up his dream history. There had been seven dreams a night, with data flowing freely. On many nights, the hit ratio had been huge, and as the database had grown, Daaisi had become better at recognising subtle differences. Pink, not red, an arched window, not a square one, the crunch of walking on gravel, not the whisper of sand. Daaisi had recounted the distances of objects and the interpretation of textures.

Eugene had added more intelligence around focus and depth perception to enhance this and had given Daaisi a voice, thinking well beyond his own interaction.

***

Lem had just sat quietly after Joost left. He knew he wouldn't make any peace with the night so didn't try to sleep. He just couldn't face what his dream's had in store. From the table Lem, saw an eerie light glow in Mollie's room.

Then he was greeted with a loud effect trumpeted in the dark. This sound he recognised as the traditional computer generated *'Ta Da'* signalling an incoming email. The noise had broken in the apartment like a freight train passing a crossing, destroying the deafening silence before hurtling off into the night and leaving a peace for ever shattered. How had a house that had such laughter and joy fallen so quiet when one of the parts of the sum departed.

Lem took a moment to let the quiet blend back into the darkness. As it slowly cleared from the space around his chair, he wriggled the fingers on his right hand to get some blood flowing. It had been a few minutes since Joost had left, or was it a few hours?

Lem drew a fist and flexed his right arm at the elbow. The table creaked as he pushed his full weight onto it and lifted himself into the air. He moved towards the closest wall and flicked on the light switch.

The brief flicker was swallowed by searing white as the room came alive. He turned and headed towards Mollie's room.

The smell that lingered in the room was still hers. He sighed, but not wanting to be lost in the moment he perched himself on the chair and inspected the computer screen which waited patiently. Lem wasn't unfamiliar with technology. He knew Mollie kept no password on the machine, so with a swipe of the mouse, the email programme presented itself to him.

It was a request for a manuscript from her publishing contact.

He looked carefully at the request. The title was 'Hodgkin's Manuscript Edits'.

Lem turned and looked at Mollie's desk. She was so neat and tidy. There was a folder on the desk labelled neatly in her hand, 'Hodgkin's Manuscript'.

Lem rose, closed the door and turned off the light before heading back to the lounge. He moved through the apartment quickly, flicking off the light in the dining room and leaving the house in darkness.

The night was cold, Rotterdam style. A strong, frozen wind rose from somewhere off the North Sea. It curled into places it shouldn't, opened things that were closed, and sliced inside with the ferocity of swarming needles.

Lem hadn't thought very hard before leaving the house. He certainly didn't consider fashion options and had walked out in clothes he generally only used to hang around in. The jumper that he wore was warm when it was worn inside, but it really wasn't up to the howl of the outside wind. He jammed his hands into the pockets of his corduroy trousers and pushed straight into the wind.

The cold numbed him further.

Lem was going to walk. He didn't know where, but he needed to find rhythm for his thoughts.

Rotterdam was a bicycle town with long, straight boulevard streets, built to ride around in. Lem didn't have the balance as a kid, so he never learned. Mollie liked it that way, as without a bike, he was hers to care for. They used the trams and trains a lot. When he had somewhere to go, she would be there to buy his ticket, make sure they made the timetable, and ensure they got off at the right stop. Lem wasn't usually allowed to walk alone and never at night, but here he was.

No one to stop him now.

Lem walked out past the Markthal and along a canal, the streets all looked the same, and he continued blindly. Left, because a car was coming to the right. Then right, towards a small park. He knew where he was but gave no mind, criss-crossing the many streets until he came to the Kralingse Bos. He would come here with Mollie a lot for ice cream.

Never again.

So he walked on.

Lem had no feeling, so as the wind howled, he let it crash against him, absorbing its pain as if he had none of his own. He walked on through the Bergse Bos and the golf course at De Rotte. At Zevenhuizerplas, he stopped He was tired.

He sat quietly on a bench on the boulevard and looked out over the water. It was quiet and lifeless. Lem felt like part of the surroundings, invisible, camouflaged. He sat for a while until his thoughts came pounding in, first thoughts of his childhood, then his future, then what he had seen today.

All of it was too much, so he got up and walked again.

While he didn't care, his choice of apparel was again working against him. He had left quickly in house shoes, not really made for the hours of street walking he had done so far or whatever lay ahead. The small blister on the inside of his foot pulled at his attention, annoying him and distracting him.

Still, he walked on.

The first glow of sunrise from the horizon was shrouded in a thick mist. Lem didn't recognise where he was. He peered through the mist, sizing up the city limit sign.

'Gouda'.

Lem didn't know distance very well, but he knew that was a long way. His right foot was searing in pain from the blister, which he thought must be bloody inside his sock.

He pushed on along the canal and saw in the distance the great golden arches of a McDonald's. Lem pulled his hands from his pockets and reached into his back pocket, where he always kept his wallet.

Empty

He now realised how hungry he was, how cold he was, and how lost he was.

The Golden Arches were a great beacon, but Lem also saw another sign.

"Gouda Station."

He could feel his chipkaart around his neck, where Mollie always made him keep it.

So he could always get home.

The sun didn't so much rise in Holland in winter, as provide an eerie light. As the day broke the clouds didn't radiate or shine they just hung like damp grey sacks.

Lem turned past the cinema into the underpass and came out at the station with questions. For the first time in his life, he would have to answer them. He swiped the chipkaart in the terminal and got on the Rotterdam Centraal train.

It didn't seem much of a first step after so many, but here he was.

***

Joost rang the bell again, without amplifying the effect he pushed the apartment bell a little harder. Silence replied again, grinning in the still air.

He had woken up early, fretting slightly about what he might find at Mollie's apartment. He had never imagined life as a priest might bring him into contact with so many difficult situations. Joost was spiritual and joined in to speak to God. He wanted to help people interpret God's word, not clean them up.

Unfortunately, if you are trying to stoke the fire, you may get burned or a least a little singed.

He waited patiently, listening for any stirrings as a pushbike whirred past. Joost didn't hear it coming but heard it vacate for what seemed like an eternity. Leaning back and looking directly at the window to Mollie's apartment he called out.

"Lem!! Are you in?"

Silence replied again, this time with a more grim expression.

He rang the door bell again.

Joost knew Lem to be a difficult kind of guy. He would be likely to not respond just because it didn't suit him or because he was busy doing something else. Joost could not assume that something had happened to him. He was positive enough within himself to assume the best, and so after waiting another five minutes, he turned and began to head back to the church.

Joost began the short walk up the street towards Centraal Station. The wide avenues were gloomy, but the air was crisp and the wind was not too strong after last night's howling gale. Joost loved the way the pushbikes ebbed and flowed along the boulevard. The noises would move from a whisk to a whirr, some provided a shudder and others a crisp, clean rubber on the road sound. Joost had always loved the freedom a bike entailed, like it was part of his soul.

He was taking particular notice of a funny-shaped rider on a very classic Dutch pushbike. The rider was very spherical and dressed entirely in black, without exception. They even wore black, dark sunglasses, which were hardly useful in the Rotterdam morning and, if anything, a bit of a self-imposed disability. The rider wasn't awfully stable, as if the sphere had cavities on one side, which unbalanced the rider, and forced them to compensate with a strange left-motion riding action.

Joost smiled to himself.

His attention turned left, and who should he see on the other side of the road but Lem?

Rotterdam wasn't a huge city, but it still felt unlikely he would bump into someone he knew. Joost signalled to Lem, but Lem must not have seen him, as he continued trudging up the street.

Joost noticed that Lem walked with a bit of a limp and was very poorly provisioned, even if the weather wasn't its usual torrent of howling wind.

"Hoi." He shouted.

"Lem!" He signalled with his finger, as if he were trying to make a point or flag down a taxi. Lem pushed on up the street in total ignorance.

Joost picked up his speed to try to weave his way across the street and catch up, but he wasn't quick enough. An avalanche of bikes burst past him in a flurry of colour and sound.

"Excuus!" cried a tall, thin blonde girl. Her bell echoed into the distance as Joost firmly planted himself on the pedestrian island.

Lem wasn't hurrying, but Joost was mindful that he might soon turn, and worried he would then lose him.

The cars quickly filled the gap once the bikes passed. He just couldn't find a break.

Finally, the green pedestrian walk signal flung into action, and the familiar tick of the pedestrian crossing gave him a starters-gun reaction.

Joost hared across the street, focusing on Lem's hunched figure in his faded turquoise jumper loping up the street.

"Hoi, Lem," he cried. There was no reaction again from his quarry.

Joost could see Mollie's apartment come into view. He didn't feel he needed to run, as it was clear now that Lem was headed home.

Another bike swished by, a long knitted multicoloured scarf trailing in the riders wake.

"Hallo Lem," he announced.

Lem was feeling through his pockets, looking perplexed, but turned and grunted at Joost.

"Stupid," he murmured.

"She would always be home to let me in. I never needed them before." Lem was clearly distressed, but the words made no sense.

"I saw you up the street, Lem," Joost explained, but Lem was lost in his own predicament.

"Just now, I cried out, but I think you didn't hear."

"Yes!" Grunted Lem. "How am I going to get in now?" He pleaded.

"What's wrong, Lem?" Joost inquired with the maximum empathy employed in his voice.

"No keys," said Lem. "I never needed them before". The corners of his lips turned down ever so slightly. Just enough to break Joost's heart.

"Oh," he sympathised.

Joost sighed at the many steps it would take to get Lem to become a part of this world.

"Can we ask Michael?" He will have keys for all the apartments in this complex.

Lem didn't know who Michael was. He didn't take much interest in Mollie's friends but drawled out a quick "OK."

Joost pushed the '*super*' button on the apartment keypad, and a friendly voice answered quickly.

"Hallo!"

"Hallo, Michael. We need access to Mollie's apartment today," said Joost. "Can you help?"

Joost had never had tea before he joined the priesthood, and he still didn't drink it. But he had become an expert at making it. It seemed that no matter where he found himself, the ability to make tea was the minimum benchmark of his worth.

They had gotten inside quickly, thanks to Michael. Lem had pushed through and was now sprawled uncomfortably on the corner lounge chair. Joost had taken the liberty of following him and took the initiative to make Lem some tea.

He found a neat set of keys on the hook in the kitchen and went to try them on the front door. They were the ones, and he returned to the lounge to hand them to Lem.

"These are yours now, Lem. You'll need to look after them and carry them with you whenever you leave the house."

"Yes, I know," said Lem.

"Would you like me to keep a set, in case you forget?" Joost inquired thoughtfully.

"If you do forget, we can call on Michael again, but I think that may run a little thin very soon. He didn't seem happy about having to provide access today."

"I will be OK." Lem said, "Mollie gave me keys before."

Joost was happy to hear that, he really didn't want to be Lem's keeper.

"OK, that's great, Lem." Joost smiled warmly. "I'm always here if you need something."

Lem looked up completely lost and turned his head to peer forlornly into space.

The silence was punctuated by the whistle of the kettle. The steam pulsated from the spout to announce its arrival at the boiling point. Joost gathered up his expert skills and completed his tea-making tasks quickly, presenting the steaming cup to Lem.

Lem looked at him blankly.

"I don't drink tea."

Chapter Three

Suffering for you, my love

Paige wasn't in the mood. Riding the underground was always a bewildering assortment of experiences. Sights and smells, late trains, overcrowding, or worse, an empty carriage with you, and London's gift of exotic weirdness riding in the seat next to you. Paige wasn't fazed, but of all the experiences in London, the underground was the worst.

She had moved back to London to escape. From the outside, it had worked.

She had a good life working in marketing for a quality interior design company, even joining the management team. She had become well respected in her field, financially secure, and externally balanced. Leaving Eugene had been a good move and helped her progress in every way. Well, that was the line she sold her friends, and it seemed to be going well. She went about her daily life like nothing had happened. She was never one to get up early, so she slept in as long as possible, washed, ate, and made it out the door with the absolute minimum of time to make her destination.

She was also pretty happy to be late.

It used to infuriate Eugene, but now she had the reins.

To wash her life clean, she spent just enough time with each group of friends to appear social. Never too close, never too distant. She wouldn't open up about anything too little or too much. Too little raised suspicion, too much led her where she didn't want to go. Time, she told herself, would take care of it all.

She tried so hard to let the weight of the past fall. She'd taken, or hinted at, enough lovers to look like she was moving on. She never kept them very long, but she never explained that in detail to anyone. It just didn't work out. He snored, she scratched, and they were way too overbearing. It wasn't hard to come up with something believable, something they'd swallow without looking too closely. She knew it was better this way.

From down train the smell seemed to course its way into the carriage before the source.

Paige retched slightly.

The warmth of the carriage interior seemed to act as a conduit, allowing the odour to invade every available space and cauterise the clean air.

The source shuffled into the cabin, sighing loudly.

Paige glanced left, a quick scan of the vacant seats. She smiled internally, as the carriage was mostly empty, with the majority of seats around her occupied. With any luck, the odour would place itself as far away as possible.

The green great coat of the source had faded like a concert poster trapped under a bridge, forever advertising what was once relevant but had long since passed. Faded, but not through being washed too often, more through exposure. She couldn't make out the face of the source through the hat, the beard, the scarf, and the dirt.

She didn't look long, it was very dangerous to engage. The source shuffled past her seat and moved up the carriage.

Paige sighed softly.

"In time," the source growled. "You will get there in time."

Paige froze, one hand still clutched around her bag strap.

"There is a future. But each must allow their path to be followed. And right now, yours doesn't lie together."

She turned slightly, just enough to glance to see if the words were aimed at her. She didn't turn too much and certainly not enough to make eye contact.

"You can always go back," the source continued. "He will always love you. You just need to reach out."

The source coughed deeply. Then gave a croaky chuckle.

"To infinity and beyond plus one."

Scuffling on, the source scrunched down into the seat at the upper end of the carriage. The odour continued to permeate, and a few of the less brave in the commuting group moved through the lower end exit to the next carriage.

Paige's head was swimming with the smell, surely the words weren't for her. There were fifty people in the carriage at the time but the context of her thoughts aligned so perfectly to the source's mumbling. She did have a habit of hearing what she wanted to hear, but what was that last bit?

Did that thing really just say "To infinity and beyond plus one."

Your path doesn't lie together. She told herself again, echoing the sentiment of the source.

She had read about what he had done since she left. He didn't say a lot about himself out there, but the dream community on Reddit was abuzz with his efforts. She scanned the Internet constantly, looking for news.

Excited but nervous.

Before she had met Eugene, Paige's first and only long-term relationship was in the final stages of destruction. It was physically devoid, emotionally compromised, and had reached a stage where every conversation was the continuation of a previous argument and every argument had morphed into one. She had wanted it to end, but it just wouldn't. She and her ex-boyfriend had each made decisions to get further away from each other and then agreed in their absence to get closer.

Then Eugene turned up.

At first, she didn't think much of him. He was clearly very clever. His abilities in logic and reasoning, and his clarity, were seemingly endless. He was so well read in history, economics, science, music, and literature. Even despite of all that, he was funny, in a warped sort of way. Quick-witted was probably closer to the mark. He could retort with something very insightful, like it was part of the conversation. He didn't seem to think about it, or maybe he thought faster than everyone else.

She liked that part.

She found herself trying to spend more time with him, and the effort was returned. It started with coffee. Conversational coffee, high-degree discussion-based coffee. Surprisingly, the conversation was not about science, or history, or music, but was always about her. He was also a good listener, she very much liked that.

But she didn't really like coffee that much.

They would talk, it seemed like they talked about nothing, but when she left those conversations, she found herself wanting to make them longer. She found he had answers to her questions, solutions to her problems, experience with her naivety, and seemed to understand her. That was it, over and above everything else he seemed to instantly understand her.

Paige had never really spoken to someone who was that much older than her as an equal before. Other people his age were friends of her parents and were more often than not talking down to her or condescendingly asking her what she was doing with her life. They would formulate those questions to set her up to fail.

"My Jenny is studying law, what was your major again?"

"My Billy just got a scholarship, how do you manage to afford your school fees, dear?"

She hated talking to older people. They always wanted her to be doing more than she was, even though she barely coped with what she had on her plate. But he was different. Gentler, more patient, and more accepting. She found herself at home, thinking about him. Not in a crude way, just in a dreamy way. That was her.

She was a dreamer.

The smell emanating from the odour overpowered her reminiscence momentarily. Her physical reaction had become overwhelming, and she just had to move. There were three stops to go, but as the train pulled up to the next station, she waited tenaciously for the train to slow.

"Mind the gap!" she was reminded.

The platform was bedlam as usual. Paige looked imploringly into the eyes of the people trying to get onto the carriage she was getting out of, but there was nothing she could do or say. They were all meat for the grinder, a heaving part of London's great unwashed.

Paige slowly and patiently pushed her way through the crowd to the next carriage and joined the queue of people trying to get on. The underground could move from free and easy to chaotic logjam in a heartbeat. Station to station, line to line. It was funnelled pandemonium.

Yet to be free of the odour, or at least the memory of it, she shuffled forward. Maybe there was no escape as the smell seemed to have taken up residence in her clothes, her nostrils and her brain. The people in front filed in slowly, she could see them moving and willed them on with quiet desperation. The conductor's whistle blew as she crossed the threshold and scanned the carriage for a seat.

Nothing.

With two stops to go, she would stand, happy to be finally free of the overpowering constriction in her throat from the source. The train pulled away from the platform, and the carriage of people flopped around like washing on a line in the undulating breeze.

The people standing next to her were trying to speak quietly, but the close proximity of the carriage meant that no matter which way she directed her thoughts, Paige couldn't avoid their conversation. The mother was distraught. The daughter was disinterested. The subject wasn't clear, but the disparity of involvement in the conversation was. She had had plenty of those conversations and tried to zone out.

The turning point from 'he's nice' to 'he's more than nice' came when Eugene let go. He always had a calming but persuasive style. Forceful but not pushy. When he asked for something, there was a yearning to act, not because he wanted it but because you felt you should do it. That day, the conversation turned to her family. Her father had disappeared again, spending time with his girlfriend, leaving her mother to pay the bills and keep things running. She had fought with her mother about, well, everything, but on this occasion, something trivial.

Paige explained the disagreement to him, and his reaction was not what she expected.

"You should listen to what your mother is actually saying, not the words she says. She is saying she loves you. You'll miss it when she is not there to say it anymore."

She just didn't expect that. She always thought he might be a bit feeling-less, but clearly not. Worth digging a little deeper. The two of them started messaging, a lot. She scratched a tarnished coin and found gold beneath. That was enough to get them started.

The train jolted on as it careered left around the curve. The conversation between the mother and daughter had retreated to a frosty silence. Time passed glacially in the reality of the underground setting, but Paige found warmth in that memory.

Their conversation had no boundaries. Time, manga, experience, history, feelings, travel, geography, the arts, dance, anime, family, music, taboos, they were all on the table. He listened and seemed to understand her so very well. He didn't try to change her, he didn't seem to judge her, he just listened. It was platonically perfect. She really enjoyed his company, and in stark contrast to her home situation and the constant battles with her family, he was an oasis. But Paige always knew her time in Holland was limited.

Then she spoiled it.

It was a warm Rotterdam day, rare in itself. They had agreed to meet in a small intimate cafe just off the canal. It was the first time she saw him in a pair of shorts, she immediately noticed the definition of the muscles on his legs. They were spotted through years of sun, scratched and burned, with patched and unstructured hair. The definition wasn't honed through months in a gym like she had been used to, it was raw and hardy, strong and real. Driven through years of adventure and life.

She saw it and she loved it.

It started there, and it wasn't long before she saw the rest of him in a different light. The physical, the conversation, the intensity, all kind of took her by surprise.

The memory was broken by a loud speaker. "South Kensington Station, change here for the Circle and District Lines."

"Mind the Gap!" The banality of the call didn't fit the memory, but Paige persevered, allowing herself a moment to search desperately for a reason.

The light streamed underwhelmingly from the day outside, like the day knew the mood that the underground swathed Paige in.

This day, her day, was like any other, and she made the walk from the underground station to the office in quick time. A wave amongst the sea of people that walked Old Brompton Road, she entered the office building quietly, ready to accept the fate of another day.

Paige took the elevator to the third floor.

"Third floor." The synthetic coldness of the automated voice always sent a shiver up Paige's spine. She moved quietly to her desk, avoiding contact with any of her co-workers. Just not in the mood.

Noticing it was empty, she slipped into the tea room to make herself a cup. The job complete and with her lemon, verbena, peppermint, and chamomile tea in hand she plonked at her desk and fumbled over some designs.

The morning's events left her with nowhere else to turn her mind. What did the odour say? "You will get there in time."

Is that the same as 'one step at a time'?

Her dream last night was time-oriented. A clock spinning, her life standing still while so many lives swirled around her, repeating again and again: children born, growing, ageing, dying. A procession of weddings and funerals, school and work, breakfast, lunch, and dinner. People she didn't know passed through time while she waited and watched. An eternity passed while she stood still, with that boy standing silently next to her.

How did a homeless stranger make that connection? Was it just a coincidence? They say a lot of strange things that never seem to make sense. Eugene always said all things were connected, lessons of fate, and you have to listen hard to know what to hear.

The two of them had spent so much of their time together discussing each other's dreams. Their relationship didn't have the easiest start, so quickly, for both of them, dreams were common ground.

Broken, erratic, harsh, and hurtful ground, but common.

They would discuss them for ages, over text, over stolen moments, and over time they had together. It all seemed to be a rush to get the information out for her, so he could listen and make sense of it. In turn she listened to his precise recounting and gave her impressions, her feelings. He seemed to appreciate the input , revel in the feelings so many would want her to push away.

In those early days, he used websites to understand, working through every detail of dreams. He was amazed at how much detail she could remember from her unconscious, and his waking mind gathered all that she could muster and processed it. The more she gave, the more he could tell her about what was going on in her life and what each thing meant. Then they would discuss those things, and in time, his insight helped her clarify so many of those things. not all of them, but to her it was invaluable.

She smiled fondly on that memory, happy times in dark shadows.

They built on that slowly at first.

As the relationship became physical, they spent more time together, and the period from dream to interpretation became instant. They didn't dwell on any meanings, they were happy to be curious and content to understand the moment. Weeks turned into months. They travelled together and found the time on the road helped to consolidate that bond. At the time, she thought it would be forever, and she thought he did too.

Dreams would come three and four times a night. Some of her dreams were so vivid, explicit, and menacing. Warnings of the past and trepidation towards the future, and Eugene would listen patiently to her recount and then lay meaning to them in all their ugliness. Then love her for it, love her complications, love her darkness, and love her complete difference from him.

She recalled when she visited him in Rotterdam and he first introduced the Dream AI. Only Eugene would trust artificial intelligence with his dreams. His first experiments were just on himself, vocal recounts of his dreams interpreted by his AI and explanations divulged on a prompt.

She hated it.

Recounted dreams with him had a humanity about them. It wasn't clinical, it was an emotional experience. The only good part of the AI was the energy and vigour that Eugene put into it. She loved to sit and watch him work through things. His shining intellect on display. But all good things must end. Fatefully, as it turned out.

"Paige?" The peace and reflection were broken.

"Where are you?" Grace was annoying and a shocking gossip.

"Just thinking through the Turner account." Paige lied badly.

"Sure," snorted Grace. "I could see Turner written all over your face."

"Plus, you have the North Shore account on your screen." Grace rolled her eyes scornfully, as if her discovery had proven her dominance in all things.

"Can I help you Grace?" Paige replied with her best business-mannered voice.

"Chuckles wants a word," Grace guffawed, "and he seems in a spiteful mood."

Just what Paige needed to top her day was a run-in with one of the directors. She rose and moved slowly and purposefully towards Charles' door.

***

The lightning burst a streaming pulse, cradling across the sky, illuminating the darkness, electrifying the clouds. The clouds wept long, bewailing tears, which played a drawn-out lament on the tin roof.

Walking quickly past the slit parapet towards the huge oaken door at the end of the hall, my heart quickened. I didn't recognise the building, and the atmosphere presented a tense dominion.

The door was always locked, but I tried it anyway.

It was locked.

I turned back and looked along the passage that I had just come down. Lightning cracked outside to produce a cloned shadow through the slit of each parapet along the hall. The shadows danced manically, then fell slain to the floor, like memories of beauty once caressing the night.

With the light gone and unable to see, I slowly moved back along the passage, touching the walls to gain familiarity with my surroundings. The walls crumbled as I made contact, the castle walls made of gingerbread dissipating further with each drop of rainfall.

I pushed my way through the wall into the empty hotel reception.

"Hello," my voice echoed, frolicking its way over the cavernous space to the oblivion beyond.

"Hey handsome!" Her familiar voice came from behind me.

"What's a nice fellow like you doing in a place like this?" Her voice calmed me, waiting for a response to the question.

I smiled and tried to answer, but I couldn't hear the words I said.

"I'll meet you there, just get the key from the desk," she said, like it was the truth.

Lightning cracked again, hard across the sky. I flinched and reached up to protect myself, delusional in my belief that my petty actions could defend against such awesome power. I looked back to where she was, and she was gone. I opened my mouth to call, but again couldn't hear my own words.

I quickly turned back to the reception desk. A big red lamp sat in the middle of the desk, with a large silver hand bell at rest on the desk beneath it. The wooden handle of the bell was smooth from over use, but the bell was polished and glorious, like it was made yesterday. I grasped the handle and shook the bell to extract the maximum sound but I was greeted with silence.

I waited patiently, counting time to the hum of the rain on the roof. After a while, I picked up the bell again and shook it a second time. No sound emitted again, and I turned it upside down to find the bell had no clapper. The receptionist cleared his throat and shot me a disapproving snarl.

"No need to ring twice sir."

"The young lady said you would be along. Here is your key, simply follow the path to the left, and you will find your way to her."

Before I could question the receptionist, he was gone, melted into the shadows that played on the walnut walls of the reception area.

I turned and looked left.

A long passageway presented itself, with rooms on either side. I started to move that way, unable to lift my feet more than a shuffle. The carpet felt like thick, sodden grass, but hoping to see her again, I did as instructed.

I pushed hard to the left as the passage broke away. The lightning had subsided, but the rain had increased, drumming a steady beat on the roof like a march to the firing squad. The feeling of dread was amplified by the next left, a long, sweeping corridor that seemed to again turn left.

Like a lost sheep, I had bleated her name repeatedly but received nothing in reply.

"Please," I whimpered, "don't go."

I called her name again but couldn't hear my own voice. The beat of the rain drowned out everything. I shouted louder, then louder and louder. I shouted so loud that I woke myself up in a sweat.

***

"Anyway, I was hoping you could help me with what that means. I know you have some experience with dreams. It was so vivid, so real, and yet so improbable."

Charles could be exhausting, but Paige needed him onside, so she listened, painfully, to his rambling.

She put on an expression of concern, leaned back, and asked. "So beautifully narrated, but who is the girl?"

"Well, I just don't know," he replied.

"Well, I would keep an eye out for her," Paige quipped, "I'm sure the dream is nothing to be concerned about. Perhaps the poor weather we have been having is coming back to haunt you, and maybe a long-lost love you just can't forget, but I have a lot on, if you don't mind."

She left him mid-plea, her thoughts already spinning elsewhere.

"Maybe you can think about it, we could meet up later for a drink..." Charles' voice echoed behind her as Paige pointed her index finger upwards as neither a positive nor a negative response.

The exit to his office had never looked so good, and Paige quickly made another tea then headed back to her desk. If his dreams were correct, his mental state was not good, and there was a likelihood he wouldn't be around for much longer. Unfortunately, she had heard of that hotel before, the parapets, the rain, and the lightning were all too familiar. He had clearly lied about the girl, and if Grace's gossip was correct, she was Belinda from the Turner Group, whom he had been seeing for about ten months but who was struggling to nail him down.

Paige had seen it before, firsthand. The connections between past and present, dreams and reality.

To anyone else, it might have seemed disconnected, but she knew better. The noise of the dreamworld never came without echoes of truth.

These connections were some of her and Eugene's first meaningful observations of dreams. They would have similar dreams, or dreams in similar places but from opposite points of view. He might see her in a car, and she would see him standing by the road while driving a car. She would visit a place, and he would go to the same place at a different time.

These were his first insights into stimulation, and by recognising its potential, he pushed his own mind hard to prove his theories.

Eugene had found that if he stimulated his brain with images, sounds, music, or smells during the waking hours just before sleep, he could influence the dreams he would have. He would use colours at first, then images, then specific coloured images. He did all the early experiments on himself with great success. He was excited to send her those successes via text message and more excited when they were together to show her the results.

She was nervous because he was experimenting on himself, but she was excited along with him.

He didn't tell her the downside, that the stimulation was also leading to a breakdown in his conscious reasoning. It was so hard to tell with Eugene, his shining intellect seemed unaffected, and so he always appeared to have the right answers. So the effects were something he could hide well.

To the few people he interacted with, he was just himself.

The stimulation had produced something in his dream he wouldn't or couldn't tell her. The conversation drifted away as he took her to a point and stopped. Something he had never done before. Everything they discussed previously had an air of openess and was undertaken with great fluidity.

As time passed he seemed to spend more time conversing with his AI and less time discussing things with her. He no longer interpreted her dreams with tenderness, just cold, clinical detachment, sometimes placing her not as his partner but as a subject in conversations with the AI.

"Paige!"

Reality stepped in to interrupt her reflection. Charles had a habit of breaking more than just trains of thought.

"I need figures, not elaborations," he said, holding high a colour-printed copy of her last report. "Graphs are based on facts, not wordy summaries. Summaries are supposed to give a summary, not be the content."

Paige took a breath. Thinking about yesterday just wasn't going to improve today.

Living for the moment, she faced down Charles and his clunky criticisms.

Chapter Four

Trivialities

The light flickered, dragged kicking and screaming from its slumber to perform. Dust particles jumped and jived in from the darkness, showcasing their unchoreographed steps in the eddy of movement the room was soon to enjoy.

The elevator doors opened, and Eugene stood, taking shallow breaths waiting patiently for some air flow before exiting. The second floor was always dusty, and nothing he seemed to do could stop it. Old buildings seemed to take on a personality of their own, and as much as he had modernised the interior, the existential charisma remained.

The second floor didn't have the same flare as the rest of the dream bakery. It was purely functional. Today Eugene had to store version eleven of the dream interceptor. He had a very particular storage method, meticulous in his filing of components, almost to match Daaisi's storage of data. That way, when he needed to go back to test a bug or salvage some parts, he knew exactly where to go.

"Daaisi," he croaked. "Begin dust extraction, second floor."

"As requested Eugene, Dust Extraction Routine 371g commenced." Daaisi's voice melted across the silence of the second floor.

Eugene stretched as he made his way along the hall. His automated cart was slightly behind him, buzzing furiously.

"Opening storage door," Daaisi's voice echoed as Eugene drew closer to the silver panel to the left of the elevator. The automated door slid open with a hiss, and another light made a staged entrance without applause.

The storage area, by default, was dimly lit. More to minimise the use of electricity and generate minimal heat than to preserve any paper or fabric that might be light-sensitive. The shelves contained large metallic-looking pods, each with a touch-screen LCD display.

Eugene pondered the decision to install touch displays.

"Open pod 3.11a."

"As requested Eugene," Daaisi's voice echoed dissonantly off the rows of pods.

The door of the pod slid upward to reveal the vacant interior. Eugene turned to the cart and picked up the first container of equipment.

"Entry of dream interceptor prototype 11a1.2 into pod 3.11a"

"Entry of dream interceptor prototype 11a1.2 into pod 3.11a, confirmed Eugene."

Eugene turned and reached down. "Entry of dream interceptor test unit 3c11.8 into pod 3.11a."

This test unit had been so well built.

Eugene wasn't shy about praising himself. He had built a lot of electronics for this project, but that test unit just seemed to keep on giving.

"Entry of components: draw 11a1.2 into pod 3.11a."

Eugene waited for the response.

"Confirmed?" he asked.

"Modification to primary cloud storage is underway. Anticipated time to completion: eight seconds."

Eugene waited ten seconds. "Confirm the reason for the cloud storage modification."

"Watchdog suspected an unauthorised examination by the cloud provider twenty-three seconds ago on the Portuguese host. Following the primary security directive, a cloud obfuscation strategy was enacted, reverting the primary cloud host to finance article 2.21f and transporting primary cloud services to a Lithuanian host."

"Monitoring of the Portuguese host will remain ongoing to determine any further compromise."

"Entry of components: draw 11a1.2 into pod 3.11a confirmed Eugene."

Eugene would take the time later to investigate the potential breach. He felt confident in the security directives that were in place and wanted to get this storage out of the way.

He didn't like to hang around the storeroom. Too many reminders, and just too dusty.

"Increase the dust extraction in the storage room on the second floor." he requested, repeating the earlier command.

"Extraction is already at its maximum rate to provide optimal comfort during this task, Eugene." Daaisi's response almost seemed to have care in its tone. Was that picked that up from her vocal prints?

Eugene had designed the systems carefully for the refurbishment of the Dream Bakery. It needed to be able to produce high-grade electronics, store them, and do it quietly. The building, like most of Rotterdam, was rebuilt after the firebombing of World War II to the best standards of the day. So when Eugene purchased the building, he could see he would need to gut it completely.

The elevators were the toughest thing to add. The look on the builder's face was priceless when he realised Eugene was serious about putting in a clandestine elevator.

Eugene replaced everything in the building. Walls, insulation, plumbing, electrical, ventilation, and even the roof, which he replicated using solar tiles designed to look like 1940s tiles. Old prefabricated walls were ripped out and replaced by mesh security walls with state-of-the-art fire suppression and security systems. Sensors were installed everywhere, allowing Daaisi to see and feel everything. The only thing that remained original was the facade and the bakery servery. From the outside, it looked like he was going to sell bread and cakes, in reality the servery made for the ideal entryway.

"Your body temperature has just decreased by one point three degrees Celsius. Would you like me to increase the storage room temperature to compensate?" Daaisi inquired. Again, with a tone that had care.

Eugene was a bit taken aback.

"Was monitoring my body temperature part of your directive?" he asked.

"Upgrades performed on August twenty fifth determined that your safety needed to be elevated to my primary directive. Decreases in human body temperature can be caused by brain diseases such as Parkinson's or multiple sclerosis, however, in your case, they are most likely due to atmospheric conditions being less than optimal."

Eugene should not have been surprised. He gave Daaisi the ability to self upgrade and make decisions based on the prime directives he had given.

"Understood, increase room temperature as required."

Eugene pondered how unfamiliar it was to have something happen without needing to make it happen. Daaisi had reached the pinnacle of the current AI technology. The perfect mimic of semi-self-sentient.

"Entry of obsolete components: draw 11a into pod 3.11a."

"Entry of obsolete components draw 11a into pod 3.11a confirmed. The status of the completed cloud move to Lithuania is available now."

"Proceed." This was also new. Eugene wasn't aware they had cloud services in Lithuania.

"The Portuguese Cloud Services provider attempted an unauthorised backup at block level. Block-level backup of finance article 2.21f was provided to avoid suspicion, but this breach of terms and conditions is in contravention of the current security directive."

Eugene nodded his agreement more from habit than any necessary physical confirmation.

"In line with upgrades performed on the 25th of August, a new cloud provider was chosen from my previously composed list of acceptable cloud service providers in countries that pose little likelihood of authoritarian action." Daaisi seemed to take an unnecessary break, more to let his brain digest the information than to gather any thoughts.

"The account was created using the main Cayman Islands company credit card, and my key functions were transported via four third-party hop points within one hundred and twenty six seconds. Further functions and data were transported in the remaining three hundred and twenty two seconds, other distributed data stores at other cloud services remain intact. All seventeen cloud service facilities remain fully operational and secure. Finance Article 2.21f will remain in place at the Portuguese facility for sixty days to avoid suspicion before the account is terminated. The report is complete. Would you like to further inquire on this issue?"

Eugene pondered the attempt. Maybe just some data monkey trying to do the right thing. He didn't like people backing up his data without his consent.

"How many years has this account been active at the Portuguese facility?" Eugene enquired.

"The account has been active for three years, two months, and seventeen days, with zero previous block backups attempted."

"Do we have any other facilities that we have had accounts at for more than three years?"

"Yes, three."

"Have there been any block backups attempted at any of these or any other facilities?"

"No, but I will review the logic in my detection code and, if required, upgrade all cloud services and watchdog services."

Eugene was naturally suspicious. Nothing he was doing was illegal, so why would anyone have been concerned?

From the moment he moved Daaisi to the cloud, he put in very strong security directives. The finance app was a ruse. At some of the cloud hosts, it fed data to other cloud hosts that acted as data services. It looked like it was reading huge amounts of finance data and crunching it to have given customers results, but really it was sending those resources to Daaisi. Whenever there was perceived trouble, Daaisi would exit the facility and move on. There were over two hundred countries housing thousands of cloud providers, and in five years of operation, they hadn't even scratched the surface. Eugene had set up a few host sites with voice services, so if someone needed phone authentication or to talk to a human, Daaisi had been there to answer and corroborate any story.

"Entry of protection band prototype 21b into pod 3.11a."

"Entry of protection band prototype 21b into pod 3.11a is confirmed." The warmth in Daaisi's voice reached a beautiful crescendo. "That is the conclusion of the storage task required. Will you be returning to the R&D area or moving to your private quarters?"

Eugene was feeling a little cold and was happy to see the end of the task. "I think I will go outside and have a coffee."

"Currently returning the storage room temperature to normal. I will direct the cart back to the research and development room."

Eugene sighed at a job well done.

The door slid open as he approached, but as usual, his gaze fell longingly to the glass cabinet by the door, his original dream journal, and the photo of Paige.

***

Eugene closed the book, deeply frustrated.

The coffee shop was quiet and the surroundings serene, but the content of the book was nothing short of annoying.

Freud saw dreams as manifestations of one's deepest desires and anxieties, strongly related to one's repressions and obsessions. Other dream analysts had given less sexual interpretations. This early thinking just didn't cut it anymore. They had a lot more tools at their disposal than just blaming the subjects mother. Whatever relationship Freud had with his mother, it just wasn't the same for everyone.

Eugene liked to read. He read a lot. The more he read, the more he wanted to read. He moved from author to author, then reading the texts of the influencer of the author, then their influencer or teacher, and so on. He read John-Paul Sartre, who was influenced by Freud, and read Nietzsche and Schopenhauer to see what Freud read. He would binge on authors and subject matters until he gained a fully rounded background. This in turn allowed him to form his own opinions, influenced, but not driven by one single thread. Often he read things that swung so drastically from the centralised conservative political and philosophical path he trod. Mostly just to see if what people wrote was rubbish for rubbish's sake or if they had a fine thread of reality initially and had just gotten carried away. Eugene read a lot of history, it was his favourite. He liked to read hypotheses and then see what the future made of that philosophy as time changed and new data came to light. Who in the late seventeen hundreds would argue with the science of Benjamin Franklin? He was a founding father and dabbling scientist, but as time went on, his basic experiments would be reconsidered and given foundation by Edison and Tesla.

In the last few years, Eugene devoted his reading to dreams. He had read Freud so many times, Jung, Johnson, Fox, and even Kari Hohne. They really did understand dreams, but they were all fairly impractical with their treatment of the dreamers. It almost seemed they were trying to stop dreams from happening. To fix what was broken. Paige would always taunt him with Jung

"Your vision will become clear only when you can look into your own heart. Who looks outside, dreams. Who looks inside, awakes. "

He liked the research papers of the Dormio targeted dream incubation device developed by Horowitz and Maes and integrated an audio module into Daaisi after reading their paper.

Eugene had a long history of dreams, interpreting them had meaning, bringing them into sync with his current waking life. But through his own self-analysis, he felt there was more to it. Eugene would experience recurring, long, boring dreams, they seemed to contain no anxiety or obsession, but they had hidden meaning in them. He liked the theory that it was his brain on a self-help decompression for the day or the week or the year. That was until he met Paige and found they sometimes dreamed similar things.

He missed Paige a great deal. For someone in his life for such a short period of time, she was an incredibly strong influence on him. Through analysing the dreams of them both, he gained far greater insight and more traction on his final goal than he ever could have on his own. Even though he wanted more time with her, deep in his soul, he was happy with the time they had together, especially as it might have never come to pass.

Eugene couldn't remember the first dream he had. He remembered fragments of nightmares as a child, but they were never over consuming, and mostly they didn't affect him that badly. More a memory of an event than a memory of any particular part of the event. As a teen, he had the usual array of erotic sensations, running to stand still, flying, and falling dreams. Again, there was little there to suggest anything untoward.

It wasn't until Eugene hit his twenties that his dreams began to become a little bit profound. He would see historical places and interact with historical people. He read a lot of history, so he put it down to his reading.

He read history, he dreamt history.

His twenties turned into his forties, and dreams came and went. Eugene had become skilled at understanding them, addressing them, and almost enjoying them. They were unscripted reality television shows. Some were disturbing, some were a little mundane, and others were difficult to understand or recall.

Eugene began recording his dreams in a journal he kept by his bed. As soon as he woke up, he would write down what he could remember. Characters, colours, objects, movements, and, if possible, whole descriptions of events and interactions.

The more he wrote, the further into the dream he seemed to be able to remember, and slowly he developed techniques to remember an increased smount of detail. Doors would become large ruby colonial doors, armbands would become amethyst-encrusted gold bracelets, water would be deep crystal blue pools or muddy insect-infected swamps. Finally, he could describe clearly purple fractals and the size of the teeth on predatory animals.

After the first written journal, as a tech guy, Eugene developed a tech way of recording his dreams. He spent years compiling and tagging dreams with keywords, and linking and caching the online interpretation or book reference to get an understanding of why he dreamt the way he did.

The history he compiled on himself was quite remarkable in itself. His first struggle was that online databases were unpredictable and variable across sources, as the people writing them were clearly always on different pathways and possibly had different motivations. The dream world is made up of many types of people. PhD students and professors, moneymakers and charlatans, mystics and romantics, and just plain ordinary dreamers.

He had to find some way of putting things in order.

Eugene started his dream database as a way to combat this chaos. He web-crawled dream sites, news sites, university sites, and pretty much anywhere he could find dream references. He cross-referenced dream instances to get probability, and for all new data, he compared this past data against the new. He added other key fields to try and shape if men and women dreamed differently, if the dreamer was rich or poor, the dreamer's location, and little things like whether they were at home or away.

Simple things that, in the mix of probability, gave him the likelihood of why he dreamt of crocodiles, or running away from his childhood friend, or why he was naked at the mall.

Eugene finished his coffee. He savoured the balanced, woody flavour and fruity aroma. As was his habit, he inspected the residue built up on the side of the cup. The sure sign of a perfect coffee was how much it left behind. This one was pretty close, as he had come to expect.

He looked up at the attendant and raised his hand. The attendant nodded in his direction and disappeared behind the counter. Eugene looked around at the busy coffee shop, feeling relaxed with senses wide open to the world.

He left the small chocolate on the plate along with the cost of the coffee and a small tip for the attendant, who had nicely put him as far away from the rest of the patrons as he could.

Making his way up the street, he breathed deeply. The road leading up to the Dream Bakery was flat, tree-lined, and an extremely pleasant walk, mostly free of traffic. Eugene took the walk briskly, it wasn't his only exercise but walking made up a huge part of his cardio and so he had to take it at pace.

Both the upper floor and ground floor high windows of the Dream Bakery had been replaced by modern toughened glass, which he frosted to maintain privacy. The frosting could be controlled by Daaisi to increase the opacity and add a light block, to block internal light from showing to the outside. The door included the same glass inset in the large black original wooden structure. The only other variation from the original was a sign on the strip above the door, illuminated by a single, wide LED to announce that this was the Dream Bakery.

Eugene placed his hand on the glass, and the door opened with a click. He pushed gently and entered the servery. The servery was the room where bread and pastries were served to customers when the building was a functioning bakery. There were benches, racks, and some space to stand. Eugene liked to keep the bakery looking like a bakery. The shelves were empty, but everything else looked like you could serve customers tomorrow, that would be if there was anywhere to make bulk bread or pastries in the building. The other key feature was a display fridge fully stocked with a wide array of drinks should anyone visiting feel thirsty.

"Welcome home Eugene," Daaisi's warm, soothing voice greeted him. "Do we have further tasks to undertake this morning?"

"Schedule three people for version twelve trials."

"Yes Eugene." Daaisi had already compiled lists to assist Eugene with the selection process.

"One strong dreamer and two low-level dreamers. Call from the student list."

"Yes Eugene. I have selected the most likely candidates. Would you like me to present them verbally or on screen?" Daaisi's voice enticed him.

"Large Screen in the Interview Room," advised Eugene as he moved through the servery.

Eugene looked over the interview list. He read through the list of dream experiences of the first student. She was in her twenties and had recurring dreams of the usual chases, falling, and nudity in public.

"Confirm test subject 232, Elsa Jansen. Make arrangements for her to attend a four-hour session. Offer her payment as part of the trial from the Dutch Bitcoin account to the wallet of her choice."

Eugene liked to pay well and anonymously.

"Confirmed Eugene. Scrolling to the second candidate."

The second candidate was a male in his thirties. Good dream history with no history of mental issues or drug or alcohol use.

"Did you cross-check candidate number 254 against police records? He has a guilty look about him."

Daaisi used a childcare charity as a front to check candidates for any sordid history. Something Eugene didn't need skewing his research.

"No criminal history was found on subject 254 Eugene."

"Scroll to the next subject." Eugene just didn't like the way he looked, and that was enough for now.

"Shall I permanently mark subject 254 as unacceptable or recycle the record for future consideration?"

"Permanently mark him unacceptable." Eugene had no shortage of candidates.

Next was a guy in his early forties, he seemed to fit the bill better.

"Confirm test subject 253, Wally De Bakker. Make arrangements for him to attend a four-hour session. Offer payment as part of the trial from the Dutch Bitcoin account to the wallet of his choice."

"Confirmed Eugene. Scrolling to the final candidate."

"Confirm test subject 257, Joss Fries. Make arrangements for him to attend an eight-hour session. Offer payment as part of the trial from the Dutch Bitcoin account to the wallet of his choice. Let's call that payment in the usual way."

Joss had a history of very particular dreams, similar to Eugene's dreams. Long, drawn-out, historical places and people he could interact with. Eugene liked to experiment with both types of people, but often this type came with a criminal history and long-term problems with drugs or alcohol. Joss was no exception.

He always needed to take extra time with these subjects. Calm them down, put them at ease, feed them, and give them time to come to terms with the task that was being put before them.

He did that so they were more likely to be receptive to the introduction of stimulation. Gentle sounds were best with these subjects, non-violent images, nothing controversial. These subjects were the true test of the dream interceptor, and so far, in his own opinion, his successes had been limited.

If he had shared his efforts with the world, there was no doubt the world would have viewed it differently.

In his opinion the world was often impressed by small things trumpeted loudly.

Chapter Five

Exigency

Eugene was born in Australia to an English mother and a German father. It made for difficult historical conversations around the dinner table, but gave Eugene a great upbringing, based on perspective.

His father didn't say much, but when he did, you quickly learned that you should listen. There were two reasons: first, he might test you afterwards, and second, because he said some pretty profound things. The second was something Eugene only came to understand later in life.

Through most of his childhood, his dad was a mysterious figure who haunted the back shed. The tests his father gave resulted in a pass or a fail. Pass was some modest praise, failure was generally rewarded with silence, which could drag on for days or weeks. There was no doubting his father's intellect, but Eugene would never understand his temperament or his motivation.

Eugene's mother was loving and kind, like she had given her life to him and his brother, as that was her agreement with the world. She did everything she could for her boys, provided great scheduling and expert feeding, and threw herself headlong into whatever pursuit they decided they wanted to undertake. She was the first mother to volunteer for oranges at halftime in a game, to sell tickets at the gate, transport the team home, or do the thankless job of cleaning up afterwards. Other parents like to pay and drop off, but Eugene's mother was immersive. She wanted to influence the quality that her boys enjoyed, not just pay for it and complain about it later. That set her apart in the generation of helicopter parents Australia produced.

Perhaps it was this mix of engaging and mystifying that made Eugene who he was.

His brother was very personable, easy to get along with, and enjoyed the company of others without the need to know everything about everything. Eugene had some of that but very early on knew that was not his place in the scheme of things.

As a kid, he would spend hours doing things on his own. Even when he was around friends, they were solo pursuits. His days were spent reading, playing video games against the computer, tree climbing, and motorbike riding. All activities where he, hopefully, didn't have to participate in lots of trivial conversation. When he did do things, it was mostly in small groups, chess, squash, swimming, tennis, or other such activities. His mother tried hard to get him into larger groups through traditional "round ball" and Australian Rules football, but Eugene just wasn't that good.

Engagement with larger groups was just something he had no interest in.

When Eugene was sixteen, his parents' relationship disintegrated. Mostly through his father's disinterest in all things and his mother's insistence that such disinterest wouldn't affect her boys.

Eugene finished school with distinction and started university, but found he just couldn't quite get excited about it. With a floundering interest in academia, he flopped for a while and after working various menial jobs to save money, he travelled. First heading to Europe and then to Asia. Eugene was a quiet traveller unlike many of his countrymen who would be loud at airports and in town centres.

He loved the old European cities like Salzburg, Edinburgh, Gent, Carcasonne, and Toledo. Somehow they hadn't forgotten who they were, whosoever had tried to make them what they weren't.

He loved the chaos of the big Asian cities like Tokyo, Saigon and Bangkok. Falling in love with Vietnam for its resilience in the face of invasion, not once but twice; Cambodia for its sadness; and Japan for maintaining its dichotomy of the historical and the modern.

Along the way, Eugene accumulated enormous amounts of knowledge. In every town he visited, he would consume the local history museums, absorb folk stories, and, if possible, get to know the local ways.

Unfortunately, the local cultures were too often re-imagined into what would make the most money from tourists for the locals. Eugene felt he understood what each town needed from those tourists. They didn't need saving or changing, they just needed a way to generate a comfortable living for their families. Not every country is blessed with an endless gold mine.

He persisted through many guided tours but eventually found himself in the museums. Dusty and unexciting to most, Eugene found them to be the true wealth of the culture. A bank where history was stored, hopefully with some truth and not just the answers according to the winners or by committee.

After a few years on the road, while his thirst for travel wasn't over, his bank balance said it needed to rest. In stark contrast Eugene's thirst for knowledge was just beginning, and so during his rest, he reengaged with university life, gaining a double major in finance and technology, before heading into the workforce.

Eugene started out working for a small oil exploration company, generating oil well probabilities. For each oil well discovered, the stock market or other stakeholder groups require the probability of the well's estimated reserve being correct. Eugene found the premise of dealing with the issue quite simple, but struggled with the bureaucratic dynamics of office bound work. He spent these years interacting with the minimum number of people necessary to get the task done, finding just a few kindred spirits along the way.

Both at work and at home, he kept himself occupied by developing AI scenarios in his spare time. AI was new and exciting, and in its infancy, it opened up a whole new world to Eugene.

His work was transformed when the research arm of the Australian Oil Exploration Company was purchased by Royal Dutch Shell. Eugene was fully expecting to be let go and was amazed when instead they asked him to move to Rotterdam to take up a research and development position in the technology group.

Never one to pass up an opportunity, he accepted.

The work for Shell was tied up in lavish amounts of process, as was the way of the highly regulated. Eugene's days were sometimes spent in meetings listening to experienced engineers, mostly talking about how much they knew, punctuated sporadically with the information he actually needed to complete the tasks he was set. If he didn't have it before this was definitely where Eugene consolidated his infatuation with coffee.

Eugene kept his brain active in his spare time by working on side projects like demystifying the financial markets. He felt there must be a way to forecast high probability changes in stock and financial markets using AI. His early AI could predict fluctuations based on web crawls, past performance, and other industry moves to within half a percent.

At thirty, Eugene quit his job at Shell to promote the software but quickly found himself involved in some regulation issues in Europe. Unsure what to do, Eugene invested his savings in the financial markets using his software as a guide.

His silent success was golden.

Eugene took the time to create a cover, some international accounts and got very good at moving money around. Creating a business that paid tax and looked on the surface to be very legitimate and somewhat successful.

While he went about his business quietly, it seems it was not altogether unnoticed, and one day he was approached by a shady someone in a coffee shop who said they represented some powerful interests who would like to get their hands on his software and make sure nobody else did.

The offer was only in Bitcoin, and Eugene was told it was wise not to refuse as it was a generous offer, not to be repeated, and that the next offer might not be so generous or in Bitcoin. All of it was said in a way that made it less of an offer and more of an offer you couldn't refuse.

So he took it.

Bitcoin was very new at the time, however, Eugene saw the potential. He was a frugal spender and didn't extend beyond his means. After sending some money back to his Mum, he saved what extra he had.

When Bitcoin rose above a thousand dollars Eugene decided not to pursue further employment. He didn't tell any family or friends, he just melted away from the work scene. His mind took on a new focus, as his dream project took shape and became his new vocation.

With a clear picture in mind of what he wanted to achieve, Eugene purchased the old bakery for a steal. It was decrepit, rat-infested, leaking, and hadn't had anyone lease it for about ten years. Its only endearing feature was its location. The owners were a little unsure of what Bitcoin was, but Eugene convinced them to do two transactions.

The ramshackled old building sold for such a cheap price, pretty much just meeting the minimum government requirement to cover Taxatierapport, transfer tax, and contract fees. A large chunk of bitcoin changed hands that day, enough to produce a big smile on the bakery's previous owner's face, even if he didn't know what he had.

Eugene set about renovating, which was no small job.

He provided his builders with some pretty formidable specifications, which kept them occupied, and in the meantime, he laid out his technology plan for dream interceptor, dream database, and dream AI.

The Dream Vision project was a labour of love from the start. The very first AI version clumsily responded to simple language text-based strings with blunt, singular answers. Nothing fancy, just getting him the data he needed quickly. He was well versed in the history of We Chat, so he modelled early versions on that simple interactive style. From there, things developed quickly, everything took shape together. Dream Bakery took around a year to complete, and by that time, Daaisi was semi-functional, although not yet vocal.

Then, by chance, as much as the world plays out, to turn him upside down and inside out, he met Paige.

***

Lem kept his left eye lid tightly shut.

He squeezed open the right eye to make sure that the sun had indeed started its journey across the sky.

His mind wandered a little, and instead of embracing the moment, Lem returned his right eye to the same state as the left.

'Not ready for that yet,' he thought sleepily.

He waited a while, letting the remnants of yesterday's events wash over him.

'If you just lie here,' he thought, 'the world will just pass you by.'

It was a good thought, and he held onto it for at least another ten minutes, until he needed to go to the bathroom.

There were very few things that returned a person to the realities of being alive, like the need to urinate. It could be overwhelming in its urgency, soothing in its relief, and most definitely worked on a timing that ordinary folk just couldn't claim to fully understand.

Lem could navigate the apartment blindfolded, but Mollie had always reinforced that he needed to pee with both eyes open, concentrating on getting the flow in the water. Even though she was gone, her voice echoed, and he faced his task with both eyes ajar. Job done, mostly successful.

Lem desperately wanted to return to bed. But his stomach had other plans and it groaned a strained lament to redirect his focus.

The kitchen was cold. Actually, the whole apartment was cold. Lem took a moment to turn on the central heating and made his way to the kitchen. He opened the cupboard and took out some beschuit, added jam and cheese, and stuffed the first one in his mouth. He made two others and added them to a plate before moving into the lounge room.

The window shades were drawn, so he moved to the string on the right-hand side. Gripping the string with one hand, he pulled tightly to get the blind to move. Obstinately, the plate in his hand ricocheted off his arm and landed face down in the carpet.

"Great!" Lem squawked loudly.

Still not one hundred percent awake, he kneeled down to resurrect his breakfast. Cheese was on jam, so the contents were not completely ruined. As the law of averages never applies when it comes to food landing upside down, Lem turned both Beschuit upright back on the plate. The remaining cheese he peeled off the carpet, inspected, and returned to the top of the jam base.

Barely finishing the first third of his breakfast, he stuffed another beschuit in his mouth and crunched down hard.

Exhausted, Lem dropped heavily on the couch and sighed.

'Coffee,' he thought.

The filter machine was within his field of understanding. He had watched Mollie use it for years. Everything he needed was in the drawer under the machine.

He slid off the couch and transported himself slothfully to the kitchen.

The coffee machine was a classic nineteen seventies yellow colour. The water storage reservoir sat on top of the main yellow unit like a guard tower on a prison wall. The filter was exposed to the right, with the final coffee jug below. The unit had two buttons on the bottom left. Power and Start.

'Simple enough,' Lem thought to himself.

He opened the drawer below the machine and found the coffee can and filters. He loaded a filter and took a guess at what Mollie's 'Two scoops' instruction on top of the can meant, spreading the scoops out as evenly as the morning would allow.

The machine let out a hiss as the 'start' light illuminated green. He hit the button and felt confident that the process was underway. He stayed to inspect and was almost genuinely excited when the first squirt of liquid expelled itself into the pot.

Coffee was a mystery and a joy to Lem. Mollie had provided it magically since he reached adulthood. Sometimes it was too bitter and needed sugar, sometimes she added milk for great smoothness, but mostly he just drank it as it came out of the filter. Today was one of those days.

The coffee popped and hissed to completion, and Lem greedily siphoned a cup from the jug, returning the pot to its cradle. He turned to make his way back to the couch and heard a distinctive 'Ta Da' from Mollie's room.

Coffee in hand, Lem sidled up to the computer on the desk inside Mollie's room. He didn't look towards the bed, he just couldn't really face the spectre of where Mollie lay in her final moments yesterday. Instead he shuffled the mouse to wake up the monitor, just in time to see the email alert disappear from the screen. He opened the email and saw it was from Mollie's publisher. The email was requesting that the Sullivan manuscript be completed. He could see the Sullivan manuscript in the open, completed folder on the desktop.

He opened the email.

.....

Dearest Mollie

I hope you are well.

I really need the completed Sullivan file returned immediately. I have tried to leave you some phone messages, but I just keep getting your answering service.

If you can't return it today, I will have to get another editor to do the job, as the manuscript needs to be returned to the client by the end of the week.

Please respond as soon as you can.

Kindest Regards

William

Stanforth & Sons

.....

Lem hit reply

.....

Dearest William

Edited file attached.

Kindest Regards

Mollie

.....

He attached the file and hit send.

The smell of the coffee lazily wafted up, reminding him that he had urgent business before the cold of the apartment transformed the sweet brew into something more sinister.

He sipped, and then took a gulp. Satisfied, he turned and went to exit the room, only to be interrupted by another 'Ta Da'.

Another email had arrived from William, which he opened.

.....

Dearest Mollie

I am so glad to hear from you. I was beginning to get worried.

This is great work, as always. I have arranged for money to be deposited in the usual way, as per our agreement.

If you can complete Hodgkin's and Hudson before Wednesday and Schpeinhardtl next week, that would be great.

Please let me know if you can't make those times or need anything.

Kindest Regards

William

.....

It seemed to Lem that William's 'kindest regards' were part of his regular email signature, with possibly no heartfelt truth included in it.

Lem looked in the completed folder, and found Hodgkins, Hudson and Schpeinhardtl were in there.

He noticed a link to Mollie's bank account was also on the desktop. He clicked and saw her account details saved on the screen in front of him. He had only needed a password and he was in.

Mollie's journal for the year was open in front of him, and her bank password was at the top, Labelled 'Bank'

He entered the digits and noticed Mollie had a sizeable amount of money in her account.

'Well,' he thought, 'it was his now'.

Her purse sat forlornly on the table, waiting patiently for her wizened old hands to take it out into the world.

As if he were taking an extra cookie from the jar, Lem looked over his shoulder to make sure no one was watching, opened it, and took out her bank card.

Ideas induced by the smell of coffee swirled in Lem's head, and a smile shimmied into the emptiness of his life.

***

Lem was not brave and never had been.

His thoughts pranced wildly as the machine whirred and ticked in front of him. He tried not to stare but found his gaze constantly returning to the camera, which dispensed stoney judgement on him.

The notes appeared first, followed by the receipt. He snatched at them, like they were going to be retracted because they weren't his.

Mollie had let him have money before, but never this much.

He turned and headed straight for the coffee shop behind him.

The experience was a little surreal. The guy behind the counter was open and friendly, but Lem didn't really know what he was doing and lacked the confidence to ask.

"Are you looking for a coffee, my friend?" the guy asked, his eyebrows twitching slightly.

Lem nodded. "Yes, please. Latte, one sugar."

"OK," the twitching subsided momentarily but picked up again during his next proposal. "Anything else with that?"

"A muffin," Lem blurted out. "A very strong muffin to eat here with the coffee."

The twitching had now turned into what could only be described as a brow pirouette. Lem nodded along with his words, as if speaking alone seemed insufficient to condone coffee and a muffin.

"Very well." The brow man gestured to the price on the cash register and after the transaction was complete to tables close by.

Lem sat in the nearest booth, nervous beyond his normal state of paranoia when he was outside the apartment.

"Latte and Muffin," the brow man verbalised on delivering Lem's order. The brow was still, possibly to let Lem know everything was OK.

Lem devoured the muffin quickly. It tasted like a muffin, and if he was honest with himself, not a very good muffin, kind of stale. The coffee was great, strong, and fruity, somewhat bitter with a lingering nutty aftertaste. He savoured it and sat for a while.

The guys at the table in the back of the coffee shop were smoking heavily. It was hard to make out who the people were, but they were laughing and joking. The music was loud, and he couldn't decipher what they were saying. His Dutch was pretty poor, but it was possible they were speaking English as well. The music seemed to get louder, and then out of the haze stepped Jez.

Jez and Lem went to the same school. The two of them had experienced many difficult interactions over the years both at school and after. In Lem's mind, Jez was a man to avoid.

Lem stood up and had to stabilise himself against the table. Jez didn't see him and went straight up to the bar and started talking to the man with the overactive brow. Lem saw it as his only opportunity to get out quickly.

"Lem!!!" Jez cried loudly from behind him, "come join us."

"I have to go." Lem said, stumbling onto the street and leaving Jez in his wake.

His vision took a moment to adjust. It could have been blind panic, or maybe the effects of the muffin. Lem really wasn't sure, but whatever it was, he had to get home. He looked unsteadily up the street in a fog of insecurity. He knew the buildings along the way, the trees, where the drains were, the bins, and the signs, but they all blurred into obscurity.

Lem stopped for a moment to prop himself on a street sign.

He had breathed heavily and so became effected by the worst of all intoxicants.

Oxygen.

Whatever the reason someone had gotten to the state they were in, alcohol, weed, pills, or stronger, they were always going to be 'fine' until they spilled out onto the street and took that first big breath. Even gasoline and sparks could coexist just fine, until oxygen was added. It was the true, indisputable, hidden intoxicant, and Lem was having his first adult experience.

He looked at the sign.

'Wait. This is not the way home.'

Bracing his focus he turned to his left and walked for what seemed like an eternity. He saw a bus stop just ahead, and in a moment of indecision, he erred on the side of a small rest, weary from the most excitement he had experienced in years.

***

Lem awoke rudely, either from the biting cold or from the noise of the bus pulling up. Given how long he had been there and the frequency of buses, it was likely the former, and he wrapped his arms around himself to gather some warmth.

Lem's head was still swimming, but his vision had cleared, and he could now see the turn to his street.

Reaching into his pocket, he felt the jingle of keys but gripped the half-heart fob that he kept with him.

He rubbed it vigorously to gain some perspective and pushed himself to his feet to make the journey home.

Chapter Six

Time and the prescription of Cocaine

"Subject 232, Elsa Jansen, is at the door, Eugene."

Eugene was still in his private rooms.

"Would you like to greet her in the servery, or shall I admit her to the interview room?"

"I will greet her in the servery. Put me through to the speaker at the front door."

"You can speak now Eugene," Daaisi said.

"Hi Elsa. I will be with you in a moment. Please come in and wait for me in the servery." Eugene waited a moment before giving the command to Daaisi.

"Open the door to admit Elsa."

"Yes Eugene. The main door has been unlocked to allow Subject 232, Elsa Jansen, entry."

Eugene made his way to the elevator and waited for it to open on the ground floor before taking the short walk to the servery.

He greeted Elsa warmly.

"Thank you for your participation in my study, Elsa."

Elsa was tall. It didn't make her intimidating, as she had a kind, gentle face. Maybe Eugene was just short, but the truth is Dutch people tend to be quite tall.

"You're welcome. I am excited to be here." Elsa replied formally.

"I have checked off all your documents, however I would like to ask again that you understand what we are going to be doing today." Eugene asked with his best serious tone.

"Yes," Else replied. "I watch some pictures, listen to some sounds, and then sleep, and you will monitor my dreams. It's just a four-hour session, right? It's just that my boyfriend dropped me off and is going to be waiting for me in a coffee shop around the corner." Eugene suspected that was a lie and quickly reflected on the sadness of a lack of trust in the world these days.

"In a nutshell," he replied with a warm smile. "Just four hours. He can wait here if you like. I don't mind."

"No, it's OK," she replied. "He has some errands to run in the area too."

Eugene nodded and guided Elsa to the first of two testing rooms in the Dream Bakery. The room had a comfortable day bed. Cushions had been added as per Elsa's request to help her sleep. The room had a few Aloe Vera plants and some occasional furniture to break up the stark white walls.

"This is the dream interceptor," Eugene explained to Elsa. "You will wear this during your sleep." Eugene presented the small white cap. "It will monitor your brain waves."

"Images will be displayed on the wall, and sounds will fill the room. You can adjust the sound by just saying 'sound up' or 'sound down'. You can also adjust the brightness of the lights in the room by saying 'lights up' or 'lights down'. The images and sounds are to guide you in your dreams and will continue to play throughout your experience. After your session, we will have a talk about what you saw." Eugene gave the instructions clearly.

"Do you have any questions?"

"No, I understand," said Elsa, fitting the cap and allowing her long, mousy blonde hair to fall down the small of her back.

"Great," Eugene replied, "I will be monitoring from just outside. If there are any problems or you begin to feel uncomfortable, please just use the safety statement. 'I want to terminate this session'."

Elsa nodded. Eugene had some early experience where subjects called out *'Stop! Stop! Stop!'* in their dreams, and he mistook it for them wanting to terminate. So he had changed his procedure slightly to put in a different safety word.

He closed the door and made his way towards the back of the Dream Bakery.

"Begin experiment 171.3.2b on subject 232, Elsa Jensen."

"Experiment commencing Eugene." Daaisi replied.

"All visual and audio to my control desk."

Eugene maintained a control area on the ground floor. It was a simple set-up with a desk and chair and several large monitors to view the whole procedure.

The experiments had changed over time, but he had meticulously catalogued the changes, even when the experiments were just on himself or Paige. Such is the scientific way.

Elsa was being shown images to lead her dreams in certain directions. Water, sand, whales, coral, crabs, and a myriad of sea creatures and scenes. She was also played sounds. At first the slow, lapping waves beating on a shore of sand, then changing into deeper water with slow whale sounds cascading through the depths.

Eugene keenly watched the monitors, watching her brain activity slowly slide into a rhythmic pattern, cascading into sleep.

Elsa moved to sleep quickly, and the changes in her biorhythms were very clear.

"She was going to be an easy subject," Eugene thought.

It was never a guarantee of clear images, but having a subject that could take in the images and then quickly sleep was a great start.

"Duplicate audio and visuals to the ground-floor kitchen."

Eugene moved to the kitchen in the very rear of the Dream Bakery to make himself a coffee. It would be a long day and part of a long week, but it was satisfying, and he was very close to some very progressive accomplishments.

The coffee fell like silk tumbling into the cup, as smelted gold might be poured.

Eugene pondered while he drank, wondering how far he had come from his early experiments. The earliest experiments were on himself and were clumsy. He spent some frustrating times trying to seed his dreams with sights and sounds. He used videos of loved ones, familiar images, soothing images, places he knew, inspiring and beautiful places, and scenes. None of them seemed to work, but through luck, he stumbled on a breakthrough. From his personal list of images, he had a great picture of the side of a glasshouse from a trip he had made to visit an old work colleague in Monster. The glasshouse was just on a picture roll he displayed, hoping the pictures of friends might influence his dreams. Instead, he had dreamt of flowers in a glasshouse. The match wasn't clear to him, but Daaisi had shown him the connection.

The EEG output had fired clearly during the stimulus and had been matched perfectly during his dream, while nothing else had. Eugene then tried simpler images, pictures of simple objects, not complicated things like people, and that was the breakthrough.

"An audio message from Test Subject 257, Joss Fries, has arrived." Daaisi interrupted in a cool, calm voice, washing over Eugene's reminiscence. "Shall I play it now or store it for another time?"

"You can play the message now." The reminiscent moment was gone, so Eugene returned to this time and this place.

"Sorry, man, I'm just not going to be able to make it." Joss sounded agitated. "Some problems with my brother-in-law's car, and he, like, my man Denny, just can't help either, and I am just going to have to go for another time. OK. Alright."

Joss wasn't the first cancellation Eugene received. Especially from the hard-core test subjects.

"Check the next available test subject and send Joss Fries a cancellation via email and SMS with a reminder that his NDA is still binding even though he didn't attend the session."

"Standard cancellation messages have been sent to Joss Fries, Eugene. Next on my list is Lem Forth. I have put his information on the second monitor in the kitchen area."

Eugene looked up. Lem looked tired and a little unkempt, maybe even a little old, but he would do.

"Confirm test subject 259, Lem Forth. Make arrangements for him to attend an eight-hour session. Offer payment as part of the trial from the Dutch Bitcoin account to the wallet of his choice."

Duplicating the images that the neural cortex flashed momentarily to a sleeping subject wasn't a natural process, and it wasn't really the initial objective that Eugene set out to achieve. He just wanted to have a better memory and overall understanding of his dreams. He read about the audio seeding of dream subjects, and though he could further that research, he started to duplicate the neural responses. Seeing his brain patterns during stimulus and then making the comparison during dreaming, so that he could replicate the image.

It wasn't an exact science when he first started piecing things together, but the AI made it better. As he improved the AI, the interpretation became a more precise process. In turn, he slowly got better at responding to his dreams, at projecting his conscious requirements through sleep, and at entering the near-conscious state of DREM sleep when dreaming occurred.

Eugene worked hard to train his mind and improve the technology. He briefly experimented with drugs but found that while using them, even though dreams were more vivid, they were less controllable, so he decided overall experimentation was better without the influence of drugs or alcohol.

After the debacle with Paige he knew he needed to widen his experiment, so he came up with this plan The research company, the forum, the non-disclosure agreement for secrecy, and most importantly, the money. Everything made it look completely legitimate and less of a plaything for his curiosity. The KVK business activities for 'Pictures of Dreams BV' showed a market research company doing research for the finance industry.

All legit and above board, tax and insurance included, paperwork all duly submitted, everything looking right to all the relevant authorities.

Eugene was also very careful not to approach the wrong type of person or anyone involved in psychiatry or dream lore. He created the Reddit forum for the public, but predominantly for students, and moderated it to find students and dreamers who fit the profile he was looking for. At first, he needed people whose dreams were particularly situational and occurred in places they could identify with. Not people who dreamed of people they didn't know or places he couldn't comprehend. He was looking for simple dreams of objects and animals.

Identifiable things.

Once he worked out the brain pattern for that across males and females and across a variety of student ages, he moved on. He would stimulate the brain with images and audio to push dreams into places so he could record those brain waves and associate the wave with the place. People were different but similar, nothing AI couldn't compensate for.

The experiments were very successful, and the wider the group of subjects he moved into, the better he became with high-quality stimulation of clean, intelligent, and pliable subjects.

He moved onto different coloured objects, an orange tablecloth, red doors, and purple curtains. He managed to elicit dreams from people, allowing his AI to push harder, turning the smallest indicators into brain patterns. He worked hard to increase the signals from the most prominent dreaming areas of the brain. He worked with iron vs. brass door knobs and pine vs. wood grain and yellow vs. tan walls. He collected data from one hundred subjects with over a thousand variations and let the AI put it together. As he moved from younger students to a wider variation in age, it began to piece together that everyone's dreams were very similar in the pattern they formed in their brains. If they all saw a red door, the pattern was the same or similar with minor variations, patterns he could catalogue and use, letting the AI fill the gaps.

It was exciting work, but as was his way, he kept it to himself. Not one of his subjects understood, they were paid to sleep and participate in dream experiments. When he was finished recording, he asked them what they saw, encouraged them to remember, and showed them pictures of what he thought they saw. Many of them saw those pictures and reacted profoundly.

After a few months, he started combining the pictures people dreamed of, rendering them into a collage of the subject, the setting, and the objects. Later, as he became more skilled, he added people to it. The final confirmation for him personally came in the work with the Felix twins, having them stimulated the same to get the same picture and differently to get different pictures. The confirmation left Eugene without any doubt he was getting somewhere.

Then, when he really wasn't expecting it, his forum lit up, and, even though he had no Instagram page, Eugene became insta-famous and was given the unofficial title 'The Dream Photographer'.

***

The hotel felt familiar.

It stood resolutely, replete in black and tan corporate livery. Marble for a ceramic price. The furniture was ageless in its replaceability, taken away at the first sign of wear to another corporate chain further down the price line.

I made my way slowly past reception. The smile of the night manager was caked on, hardened through years of coffee. Less addiction, more dependence.

The paintings on the walls in the hall were serene, a thinly veiled attempt to instill tranquility and abandon the mayhem that swirled outside. The music was uncoiled with an eclectic rhythm, almost an attempt to match the peace of the paintings, but with a variable back beat. Not the usual plastic chill music, boding a difference that should have been self-evident in passing reception.

Room numbers presented themselves gleefully, shining out the beacon of welcome, which faded quickly when it was clear that the room wasn't the destination. My room number made the same silent wave as I paused in front of the door, then remained stuck in the moment while I reached down to swipe the card in the reader.

I entered the room, which had become my home.

How long I had been here, I couldn't recall, and it just seemed unimportant. The bed was unmade, and my usual assortment of things was spread throughout. Less like a bomb had hit and more like a badger had emptied my bags. On first glance, all was as it should be, and I began to undress to take a shower. As I hung up my shorts and looked upwards, I noticed the complimentary bathrobe had been vandalised and stuck to the ceiling. Small equilateral, Pythagorean, and right-angled triangles had been cut out, leaving the bathrobe intact but offering little in the way of privacy or drying quality. The lights on the ceiling blinked a quick hello, and the music volume playing in the hall seemed to increase ever so slightly, invading the usual silent sanctity of the room. The music's back beat was accentuated, and the words dripped into the chorus.

"Stham si cisum"

"Stham si cisum"

"Stham si cisum"

My temple throbbed in time. I felt a long, concentrated ache, followed in sync by a pain that tore across my brow. The music seemed to rise up to provide the soundtrack to the din in my head.

"A shower," I thought to myself. "That will wash away, whatever that is."

"Stham si cisum," the verse, must have given away time to yet another chorus, which had annoyingly become the song.

Naked, I opened the bathroom door and was immediately struck by the towel in a similar situation to the bathrobe, except with circles and ovals cut from it, all stuck to the ceiling.

My head pounded, but I convinced myself that a shower was the cure.

I let out a brief groan and turned, looking clearly into the mirror.

"Music is Maths," the vocal came accross clearly and the back beat flipped to a perfect time giving relief to my aching head.

The music clawed to an abrupt halt, leaving quiet to flood into the space. I shook my head, still not one hundred percent sure what that was all about, and let the cool water immerse my body.

Lost in the cascade, I let the troubles flow from my shoulders, transporting my mind to a totally relaxed state.

The water screamed to a halt after three minutes as a reminder that long showers are not good for the planet. There was no doubt a card explaining the hotel policy, less about saving the world and more about maximising the profit while maintaining a 'look at what little angels we are' attitude.

I reached for the towel and was plunged back into my situation. Cut up towel and cut up bathrobe on the ceiling.

Time to call it in.

Still dripping, I opened the bathroom door to walk to the phone, only to be greeted by everyone I knew.

Family, work colleagues, casual acquaintances, and ex-girlfriends.

All squeezed into my hotel room and are now pointing and laughing at my nakedness.

***

Eugene woke up slowly.

He was usually one to get out of bed quickly but in this case he really didn't want to face the reality of a conscious recall of the dream he just had.

Living life without a regular group of friends had never bothered him. He had never lived in the wilderness and always had people to interact with. Sadly, a great deal of those interactions left him feeling fairly dejected or at a minimum sullied. This was primarily because very few people in the world saw anything from his perspective, or with his candour, humour, and precept.

He really didn't like the ordinances of others in so many aspects.

To Eugene, being alone was not loneliness, and being with people didn't necessarily negate a feeling of a lack of connection. Worse still was to make a connection, foster it, care for it, and then just see it wither as the beneficiary gave back little and selfishly and terminally twisted the relationship to something that just didn't satisfy him.

Eugene liked to look on the bright side and felt lucky.

He had a brother. A bond time couldn't strip. Something no amount of arguing, pettiness, indifference, or ignorance could separate.

He stopped to ponder his dream and just couldn't recall his brother in the hotel room.

Even thought his contact with his brother wasn't as much as he would have liked it to be, the bond was constant and strong.

A strength unsaid.

For him it was everything.

Chapter Seven

The Stimulation of Reptilia Rosea

Lem opened the door of the dream bakery slowly, still unsure if the click was for him.

"Hello," he whimpered, struggling to draw breath.

"Hello Lem, sorry for leaving you standing outside for so long. I had some trouble with the automatic locks." Eugene lied, moving quickly into the servery to greet Lem.

"Really," said Lem in an amazed tone. "You have automatic locks?"

The frenzy of the morning was finally over, but it took Lem a little while to find calm. The servery was not what he was expecting.

It was empty.

"Is this really a bakery?" He blurted.

"It was once," Eugene replied, "but we don't make anything here anymore. We just try to understand dreams."

"Oh!" groaned Lem. "I was hoping for a nice cup of coffee."

"Sounds like a great plan, Lem. There is a kitchen in the back," Eugene responded warmly.

"But I think we will have coffee after the first session. I have found that coffee can affect the results of the dream test."

Lem smiled, one of those kinds of smiles where people are not sure if he's happy or if he just knows something no one else does.

"If you're ready, we can move on."

Lem nodded in agreement, his mouth still agape.

The pair made their way through the hall and into the interview room.

"Thanks for participating at such short notice, Lem. I really appreciate you coming in."

"I have made several attempts to get an appointment. Always happy to take advantage, if someone else can't make it." Lem again smiled one of those difficult smiles.

"Are you clear on what we will do today, Lem?" Eugene enquired.

Lem nodded again. "Would you really be able to tell me what my dream meant?" Lem looked up like a puppy, asking for treats.

"In my experience, dreams are never quite that predictable," Eugene explained.

"Mine is." Lem corrected. "Generally, I only have one."

"Well, I plan to show you a series of images and play a series of sounds before you sleep, which may lead your dreams into places they haven't been led into before."

Lem nodded. "Yes, I read your information. I am ready to try."

Lem sat on the day bed, a little unsure of what to do next. Eugene smiled. It looked to Lem to be a very genuine smile.

"This is the dream interceptor." Eugene explained to Lem, as he had explained to all the participants. "You will wear this during your sleep." Eugene presented the small white cap. "It will provide biometric signals we will use to monitor your progress."

"Images will be displayed on the wall, and the sounds will fill the room. You can adjust the sound by just saying 'sound up' or 'sound down'. You can also adjust the brightness of the lights in the room by saying 'lights up' or 'lights down'."

"The images and sounds are used to guide you in your dreams and will continue to play throughout the experience. After your first session, we will have a break and talk about what we saw." Eugene gave the instructions clearly.

"Do you have any questions?"

Lem had a million questions, and his mind was swimming, but he just nodded, trying hard not to look stupid.

"Great." Eugene blurted out the word to cut the uncomfortable silence "I will be monitoring from just outside. If there are any problems, please just use the safety statement: *'I want to terminate this session'*."

Lem looked puzzled. "Why would I want to do that?" he quizzed.

"If you find yourself in distress and want the lights to come on and the stimulation session to stop, just say those words. I will come in and..."

"I'll be fine." Lem butted in over the top. "I don't want to stop, whatever happens."

Eugene swallowed his words as he finished fitting the dream interceptor over Lem's head and made his way towards the exit.

Left in the room on his own, Lem struggled to relax. His excitement had reached a crescendo. He was finally here. Maybe now he will get some answers. He heard the music start in the background.

'What is that?' he pondered. 'Are those whales?'

He wasn't good with hats and never wore one himself, ever. The dream interceptor was a little tight, and it was uncomfortable around his ears. With all the excitement of the morning, he wasn't sure he was going to be able to sleep. Lem was also a little confused. He looked at the images on the screen and let the music wash over him. The writing on the newspaper was a little out of focus. A lone oak tree in autumn and some graphs. Lem wasn't sure what they were, and his mind raced to catch up.

'Did I miss one?' he thought. 'Newspaper, tree, graph, cat, was that a rock?' He tried hard to recall, just like in the memory game he would play with Mollie.

The music had changed to wind rustling in a tree. Lem liked that sound, so he just laid back and tried to relax. He let the morning wash over him again.

'Damn that old lady to black,' he thought.

The music changed to waves lapping at the shore.

"Excuse me." Lem's loud cry cut the tranquilly of the room.

"I didn't think I would need to before, when we started, but I need to use the restroom."

The light came up slightly, and the volume of the music dropped to a minimum.

A female voice, a very soothing female voice, came across the room.

"The restroom is on the wall opposite the door you entered from. You can leave the dream interceptor on or remove it and replace it when your trip is complete. If you need further assistance, please let me know, as I am here to help in any way I can."

Lem decided to leave the hat on. It was still annoying, and he scratched at his ear as he moved towards the door.

The small bathroom was very modern but plain, and he completed his business quickly and made his way back out to the day bed. The music had reset to whales again, and the screen had a deep blue hue.

"I'm OK to start now," Lem said. "I'm very sorry that I caused the delay, but there was this person on the tram who... "

"Restarting stimulation," the female voice calmly announced, cutting Lem off.

Lem wondered who the girl was.

She had a nice voice, slightly British. He imagined her kind face, blue eyes, with light blonde ringlets cascading across her forehead. The images had started in the same sequence: newspaper, tree, graph, cat, rock. Lem could finally find some sense of relaxation and let his eyes drift closed as the beautiful sound of the wind in the trees cradled him to sleep.

***

Eugene had read excerpts of Lem's recurring dreams before through his dream forum. It was clear Lem was an interesting character, but the same could be said of lots of members of the forum. Eugene's interest peaked when Lem described the location and gave some indication of the timing of his dream. A time and a place Eugene was familiar with.

Eugene had taken his time getting coffee. He could see Lem was edgy, and he didn't expect any immediate outcome. When he asked for directions to the bathroom, Eugene rolled his eyes.

"Transfer video and audio to the control room."

Eugene had begun to allow Daaisi to interact with the test subjects for a few weeks now. He hoped it would improve the AI's articulation and ability to recognise jargon and accents. The encounters were minimal, but they were important, and Daaisi was programmed to recognise mistakes made and correct them in subsequent encounters.

By the time Lem had settled down, Eugene had just moved into his chair in the control room. The leather chair gripped him, hugging him tightly in its cold embrace.

He watched the brain patterns, seeing that Lem was still concentrating heavily and pondering something. He did seem very flustered when he arrived. Eugene tried not to get involved in people's personal lives or to engage them in conversation beyond the minimal he needed to get the testing underway. He knew some of them had psychological issues and probably should, were, or had seen doctors of all persuasions. Many of them had been suitably doped up in the past to not so much dull the experience, as inhibit the pain of their lives.

He didn't see that in Lem. The guy looked tired and jittery, but he wasn't a regular drug user, certainly not on any heavy-prescribed suppressants.

83

Lem's cognitive readings started to fade as he slipped off to sleep.

Eugene watched the indicators change as he had hundreds of times. The stimulation pattern Lem was given wasn't special, it wasn't specifically aimed at him. It was the starter pack, the one he gave all first-timers. It aimed their dreams down a familiar path, things everyone dreams of.

The responses he had gotten so far were almost one hundred percent. The expected reactions he would get would be from a childhood memory, or a favourite corner of the world, most regularly at the beach. It made the first image resonate with a lot of his test subjects, so hopefully they would agree to return.

Eugene waited patiently for Lem to enter REM sleep.

***

Lem woke up in a cold sweat.

His ear was burning and like a cat cleaning his ears, he ran his curled hand across the front of the dream interceptor to try to soothe it. The rough exterior of the plastic cap wasn't what he expected and propelled him into the moment. The lights were still low but seemed to be becoming brighter, and some light classical guitar music was playing. He waited, a little unsure of what came next. His parched throat was an immediate issue he had to quench.

"Some water," he croaked.

The lovely voice he had heard before wafted through the sterile room,

"Please remain still and calm." Daaisi said gently.

"Some water, please," he pleaded.

Eugene entered the room holding a large glass of water and handed it to Lem.

Draining the glass, Lem looked up expectantly.

"Did I do OK?" he asked.

"Yes, Lem. That was great, we got good results from the test."

Lem sighed in disbelief. He finally got something right.

"So what happens now?" he inquired.

"There is some sophisticated back-end processing being done as we speak," said Eugene in a matter-of-fact tone. "Most results take less than twenty minutes, especially on your first dream."

Lem sat upright and shuffled a bit to make a comfortable spot.

"Are you feeling okay?" Eugene asked.

"OK," said Lem, shuffling some more.

"Would you like to walk with me to another room so we can talk about what we are expecting and wait for the results? If you like, I can make that coffee for you."

"Oh Yes," Lem exclaimed emphatically recovering his composure. "That would be the best."

The pair migrated slowly to the kitchen area through the open door. Lem felt awake now and had a million questions but wasn't sure how to approach Eugene. Eugene seemed a little reserved to him, maybe even distant. Instead, Lem reached into his pocket for his half heart fob and rubbed it furiously.

The kitchen was more than twice the size of the kitchen Lem had in Mollie's apartment. The room was coloured in shades of grey and black, with a large red coffee machine as the centrepiece. 'Very stylish,' Lem thought moving around to take in the space.

"What sort of coffee would you like Lem?" Eugene enquired.

"Can you make a latté?" Lem asked.

"Coming up," Eugene said confidently. "Sugar?"

"Yes please, just the one," said Lem eagerly.

The grinder was a little noisy. The overpowering noise frustratingly broke any possibility to continue the conversation for Lem.

Eugene packed the filter tightly and fitted it into the head. Lem didn't see which button he pressed, but the machine kicked into life and coffee started to flow.

Immediately a deliciously warm, bitter smell filled the room, moistening Lem's jowls with anticipation.

After the second grind was complete, Lem cautiously inquired. "Who was the girl I heard, before I went to sleep?" Eugene stopped what he was doing for a moment and looked up at Lem with a smile.

"Does she work here?" Lem met Eugene's gaze quizzically.

"No Lem, that is the advanced artificial intelligence here." Eugene said, offering no further clue.

Eugene moved quickly around the coffee machine. Lem saw a knob turned and a button pushed, but he wasn't used to such a large machine and wasn't really sure what was done. Eugene started the milk-frothing procedure, again bringing the noise level above any possibility of conversation.

Lem watched as Eugene poured the frothed milk expertly into some very professional-looking red-coloured coffee egg cups, forming perfect tulips in both cups.

"Wow!" Lem said way too loudly, "you really look like you could work in a coffee shop."

He blushed and immediately chided himself for saying such a stupid thing.

"Thanks Lem. It's a side hobby of mine," Eugene said. A smile diffusing any uncomfortable thoughts Lem might have.

"Let's have a seat."

Lem moved to the round table and took a seat where his coffee was placed.

"Did you need anything to eat?" Eugene inquired thoughtfully.

"No, I'm not hungry." Lem replied, "So how do you make her sound so real?"

Eugene looked back, a little bit proud, of all the subjects he had shown through the dream bakery. None of them had commented on Paige's voice before.

"Daaisi is the result of many years of work. Thank you, Lem. The vocalisation is self-aware and, like us, intelligent in it's delivery."

Lem smiled, one of those grimaced happiness smiles he seemed to have perfected.

"I thought she was real." Lem blushed. "I am not very good at telling the difference."

Eugene quickly took control of the conversation. "I could see from the monitor that after the little false start, you slept quite well and dreamt for quite a while."

Lem nodded, trying to form a puppy-dog face.

"It looked like a single, continuous dream. Is that correct Lem?" Eugene enquired.

"Yes." Lem replied, "pretty much the same dream I usually have. Sometimes if I get interrupted, it can end early, or sometimes it seems to fade, maybe just my memory of it. But today it was very clear."

"My processing will show an image from the dream. A pictorial representation of the key aspects of the dream, hopefully placed into perspective based on the nature of the dream, what we know about you, and the information we gathered during the initial targeting process."

"Does the information from the hat tell you that?" Lem asked clumsily.

"Yes Lem. The dream interceptor 'hat' reads your brain patterns while you wake and while you sleep and allows the resultant image or images to be created and presented based on that combined information. It's a process that improves over continual use."

"So the more I use it, the better it gets? Will we have another try?" Lem asked.

"Yes Lem, but let's see the image we gain from the first session, and perhaps you can just relax here a bit in the meantime."

Eugene finished his coffee and excused himself.

"I just need to check a few things from your session. Please just remain here in the kitchen. I won't be gone for more than ten minutes."

Lem nodded as Eugene exited the room.

***

Eugene made his way to the control room and sat in front of his large monitors to inspect the progress of Lem's session.

The image rendering was at fifty seven percent, but he could already see from the keywords the image was being built on that it was all wrong.

"Compare stimulus data to keywords for me, standard matching."

"There is a three percent match between the detail shown to subject 259, Lem Forth, and the data returned from the dream interceptor Eugene. This is the lowest of any subject. The previous lowest was subject thirty four, John Sendtner, who returned a match of forty-nine percent."

"Three percent," Eugene exhaled disappointingly. "So what keywords were returned? Do they match anything we know about the subject?"

"Yes Eugene," Daaisi replied.

"They match known keywords from a recurring dream that the subject has referred to multiple times. I have put the data on the secondary monitor in front of you."

Eugene scanned the data. It was going to be a street scene. The car description put it possibly from the nineteen twenties or thirties. There were some strange images, things that wouldn't be possible to deal with on the first test, and gaps that would need to be filled in.

"Rendering now at seventy five percent," Daaisi broke the silence.

"Test subject 259, Lem Forth, has exited the ground-floor kitchen Eugene," Daaisi broke in.

Eugene moved quickly to the door, which opened for his exit.

The control room was at the end of the corridor around a dog leg, so he had no chance of encountering Lem at the door. He turned the corner but found the hallway empty.

"Location of test subject 259," Eugene hissed impatiently.

"Test subject 259, Lem Forth, has returned to the interview room." Daaisi replied calmly.

"He must be eager." Eugene muttered under his breath.

The door to the interview room was open, but Lem wasn't in there. Eugene didn't like to converse with Daaisi if anyone might overhear, so he looked back into the hall and took a few steps to the kitchen before returning to the interview room. Hearing the toilet flush behind him, he turned to see Lem smiling.

"I just needed to go," Lem grinned. "Are we ready for another dream session?"

Eugene was slightly annoyed but kept his indignation in check. "Soon, Lem, first we need to do some work on your picture and sound recognition."

Lem nodded and sat on the bed.

He reached into his pocket as his confidence evaporated.

"You might feel more comfortable at the table." Eugene pointed him to a small table in the corner of the interview room. "We will need to have the dream interceptor unit on for this."

"How did my picture turn out? First time I have seen that thing in my street," said Lem. "Can I see it?"

"It hasn't quite finished rendering yet." Eugene responded curtly, "Seeing as you are keen to proceed, let's get you to look through a series of images on this tablet. Each image will display for five seconds, with a break of two seconds between images. You just need to look and let your normal reaction occur before the next image displays. Try not to let your reaction run over to the next image, and try not to overthink them".

Eugene had explained this so many times, but he tried to remain enthusiastic.

"Sounds will also play, both over the images and when there is a black screen. Again, all you need to do is have your natural reaction. If it's funny, you can smile or laugh."

"Is there a test at the end of which ones I remember?" Lem asked.

Eugene was taken aback but maintained his decorum. "No Lem, the dream interceptor is recording your brain patterns when you are conscious so we can use the data for images and sounds you see when you dream. No test."

"Oh right" said Lem, grinning. "Clever, like copying."

Eugene fitted the cap to Lem and again reiterated, "Please don't leave the room while the images are playing. If you need to stop the display, just say "I want to terminate this session."

"Right," said Lem.

Eugene left Lem to ponder the images and headed back to the control room. When he got back, the image had finished rendering.

Greeting him, glaring at him from the front of the image curled around a newspaper stand, and ready to spring at him was a large pink tiger-striped snake.

Chapter Eight

Insufficient Dreams

Eugene could hardly believe his eyes.

The pink snake, the bane of his dreams, was there as an image from the dream of someone else.

"Verify the snake colour, skin texture, and size. I want to see the readings from the dream interceptor for test subject 259 on my main monitor." His mind raced through the possibilities, all of which involved some kind of error.

"Readings are displayed as requested on your main monitor, Eugene." Daaisi's attempt at a soothing voice was lost in the whirlwind of Eugene's anxiety.

"Display dream interceptor readings from my own final dream test on the secondary monitor."

"Readings displayed from your final dream test as requested on your secondary monitor, Eugene."

Eugene's jaw dropped, and his shoulders fell. The readings were identical. How was this possible?

The pink-tiger-striped snake had begun to take over Eugene's dreams, it was the reason he brought his own dream studies to a close. He wasn't one hundred percent sure what it was, he just had ideas and scattered historical evidence. Freud said it was a phallic symbol, but his dreams were not sexual in nature or context, so he had disregarded the venerable word of Dr. Sigmund. Some dream dictionaries listed snakes as a symbol of the unconscious, while others listed them as an animal of transformation or transition. Other interpretations listed the snake as an agent of hidden emotions and the need to focus on life.

To begin with, Eugene had seen the correlation between the need to focus on life, but that could be true anytime in anyone's life, and he finally discounted this as just too generic. Like any interpretation, the devil is in the details and the context. Eugene had hunted everywhere to find where such a serpent existed and found nothing, he had certainly never seen one in real life before. He had never seen such an animal associated with anything or anyone else until he dreamt about it, and, of course, now.

The colour pink in dream interpretations is usually associated with passion of some kind. Unrequited love, unfulfilled obsession, excessive care, or unrealistic expectations, although sometimes it was a connection with spirituality. So maybe this had some significance for him. As a male dreamer, pink was not common, and in all his other subjects, males would only dream of minimal amounts of pink, usually associated with women in their lives, usually wives, girlfriends, daughters, or mothers. It's presence showed a strong emotion.

Tigers themselves had very dominant positions in dreams. They showed the dreamer's strength, wisdom, and resilience. Eugene's subconscious had modified this premise and placed the tigers camouflage over a pink snake. Eugene once read that the tiger might be an unconscious attempt to display control over certain energies. Was this an attempt to hide emotion or a connection to spirituality?

Whatever its colour or shape, the snake always obscured the important details of the image his mind tried to form. This is why Eugene had to stop testing on himself because he couldn't shake this pink tiger-striped snake. As he progressed, it would be in every photograph he rendered, sometimes it would be full front and centre glaring at him or aggressively taunting him. In other rendered images, it would cover up important details or the faces of other participants in the dream.

He didn't know what it was, but he knew it blocked his progress, so, in a good scientific way, he moved on to other subjects. For a while, he thought it might be his totem, his animal, trying to tell him something. Now Lem of all people had the same animal.

"Lem!" he exclaimed, shouting out loud. "I need to ask him."

Eugene turned on his heel, composed himself, and walked quickly towards the interview room. Before entering, he curtly issued the command.

"Terminate the stimulation of test subject 259 Lem Forth, without confirmation."

He entered the room, and Lem looked up at him with a blank look in his eyes.

"Lem," he said, clearing his throat. "Can we discuss your image now."

"Oh yes," said Lem happily. "Is it finished? Can I see?"

"Not just yet," Eugene said, shutting him down.

"Tell me about the snake." Eugene whipped his words, forming the request to demand a reply.

"Yes, that was a bit strange." Lem sighed. "I've never seen it before. Everything else was as the dream usually is, but the snake at the end was something new, and it was pink. I don't usually have any pink things in my dreams."

Eugene was bewildered.

How could he not know?

"First time," Eugene muttered.

"Is it important?" Lem quizzed. "Can I see the image?"

"Yes, of course." Eugene conceded using his mobile phone to transfer the image to the screen in the interview room.

The image flicked into place before Eugene reached the end of the sentence.

"Oh, that's amazing," cried Lem. "That is exactly the snake I saw in my dream, the expression on its face is so precise."

Lem's excitement was nice to see for Eugene, but in that moment, he wasn't about to get carried away with it.

"The background is the street," said Lem. "The one I always end up in. The car in the front, I think, belongs to me, although I can never seem to drive it. But when I am in the dream, I feel some attraction to it. It's a shame the snake's tail is in front of the licence plate, or we could see the registration. That's always the detail I can't remember in dreams, important stuff, dates, numbers, street names. Look at that, the snake's head is covering the street sign too. Wow, your images are really good. I had heard they were, but now I see you really do bring what people dream to life."

Eugene wasn't really listening to Lem prattling on. He had heard hundreds of people excited at seeing the images. In previous times he had been excited by the clarity himself. But today, the appearance of the snake totally threw him.

"So what now?" Lem broke the uncomfortable silence that had spread itself over the room.

"Did I finish all the watching of pictures and listening to sounds?"

Eugene would usually question the subjects on mood and state of mind and try to elicit information that could explain the rendered images that had been produced. He couldn't get that out today and was floundering with what to do with Lem for the moment.

"The visual image and audio package display were incomplete." Daaisi's clear, calm voice washed over the room, a saviour to Eugene's confusion.

"I can proceed from the previous break point if required or restart from the beginning."

Lem looked over waiting for Eugene to take control.

"Are you sure she is not real?" he elbowed Eugene with a wink of brotherly solidarity.

"Yes, very sure." Eugene rebutted curtly.

"Yes, let's resume from the pause point. Lem, if you don't mind." Eugene motioned to the tablet and got up to leave.

"OK," said Lem. "I'm excited."

The package would last around another thirty five minutes, which gave Eugene some time to collect himself and look a bit closer into the patterns of his original dreams.

The interview room door barely slid closed behind him before Eugene issued his command without thinking.

"Search for other similar brain patterns in all test subjects to date."

"Search parameters will result in a search duration of three weeks using Bayesian search algorithms using ninety five percent of the available cloud CPU."

"Cancel that search." Eugene needed to narrow the search. But how? They had never tagged a pink snake before.

"Search only dreams tagged with snakes." Eugene clarified.

"Search commenced with an estimated response in 12 minutes."

"Put the images up in the control room," he barked.

As he arrived in the control room Eugene looked back blankly at the two monitors in front of him.

The snake glared at him mockingly.

His mind wandered a little, to the times when that snake terrorised his dreams.

The first time it appeared, he didn't think too much of it. He even laughed at a pink tiger-striped snake, only his crazy brain could come up with something that boringly bizarre. As time went on, it would start to appear in the strangest of places, covering up some of the details that he had dreamed. For a while, he thought it might be a bug in the rendering code, a replacement he had put in then overlooked.

He checked thoroughly first for the obvious, then in a line-by-line inspection, and finally by using a cut-back replacement code. As this process ensued, and the snake appeared more, Eugene's mental state became worse. He became quite good at hiding the torrent in his mind, and having a complex range of issues in front of him helped to both obfuscate and define.

The pink snake became such a regular partner in his nightly dreams, a bane in the code and a recurring terror in his subconscious. So after years of torment in his own mind, here the snake was with Lem, almost at random.

"Apart from your own dreams and Lem's dreams today, approximately 33% of subjects have reported dreams that involve snakes," Daaisi broke in.

Eugene knew snake dreams were common. Even by his estimation, a third was a lot.

"From that group, search for how many snakes were pink."

"Search has commenced and will take a further four minutes using all available cloud processing," Daaisi replied formally and efficiently.

Eugene leaned back in his chair and looked at the monitors in front of him. Lem's render gave an amazing angle with clear detail. Daaisi had found some data online on the subjects and in the absence of other commands, vocalised it.

"Pink snake dreams account for less than one percent of those recorded dreams. Some dream lore accounts record pink snake dreams as symbols of strong will, good nature, and an easy-going attitude. They highlight the need to reevaluate the situation and rethink. They can also possibly make reference to someone on some intimate level that is difficult to admit. Other discovered dream lore also provides references to new hope, growth, desire, knowledge, and life."

"Pink snake dreams are distributed evenly between males and females and follow a linear transposition across all age groups except those over 80, who appear to have 50% less recollection."

"Does Lem's snake match the pink snake dreams Paige had?" Eugene blurted out.

"The records of subject two are locked, and I require an override to access those records."

Eugene had needed to block access to her dream records less for her privacy and more for his sanity. He was pretty sure it was the same so left that for another time.

"Forget that last search." Eugene said resigned. "Search for males thirty to fifty years old for pink snake instances and show a montage on my tertiary monitor."

"Presenting the montage now."

Eugene looked at the collection of dream photographs from his test subjects. There was no correlation, the pink snakes were mostly in positions of engagement. Coiled and relaxed or poised and ready to strike, depending on the feeling the dreamer had perceived. He continued to watch for a pink snake blurring or hiding something in the images.

"Sixty-second warning on the completion of the second visual image and audio package for Subject 259, Eugene." Daaisi broke the complicated silence, untwisting his brow and bringing his focus back to his immediate issues. "Based on previous experience with this subject, he is unlikely to remain patient should he not be engaged immediately after the package is complete."

"Engage him how you see fit." Eugene exhaled without thinking.

"I have been working on several idle conversational subroutines and would appreciate the opportunity to test them further on subject 259," Daaisi replied. "My choices are current news, the weather, and sports. Based on my observations of subject 259, I don't believe he will be engaged by conversation on current news or sports, and my estimation is that any conversation I should begin on the weather is unlikely to provide more than two minutes and forty five seconds of additional time. I have also been experimenting with allowing subjects to talk about themselves and extending the conversation, as it is, by providing responses made up of a subject and an auxiliary verb or modal to continually turn the conversation back on them."

"Engage those subroutines. I will be back in a moment."

Eugene left the room as Daaisi confirmed his request.

He headed for the bathroom to wash his face. The bathroom seemed small, and the blood in his face throbbed upwards, looking for an exit through the crown of his skull.

He looked at himself in the mirror and closed his eyes.

The space inside his head swam, and without further warning, he vomited into the sink.

***

"So that was why I was a little late this morning. Those tram drivers are very sullen and moody. I would say most of them are bordering on passive-aggressive."

"Yes, I agree, Lem." Daaisi's conversational tone was at its most relaxed. "Do you catch public transport often?"

"I don't have a licence or a car and can't ride a bike because I just don't have good balance." Lem turned to see Eugene had entered the room and was smiling.

"Are you sure?" He looked at Eugene expectantly. "That is the nicest conversation I have had with a lady for such a long time."

"I'm sure!" Eugene exhaled.

"Lem, I have a few questions before we start the next session. If you don't mind." Eugene said, lowering his brow to look appropriately serious.

"Sure," Lem said, like a puppy who has spied the walking lead.

"Tell me more about the street in your dream." Eugene said, needing to go back to basics.

"Yeah. I must have some attachment there. All the dreams I remember are about that street. Sometimes I seem to be there for the longest time. I see people grow up, get old, and move around. I interact with them. Sometimes they are mean, and sometimes it's just a normal day." Lem said shifting slightly.

Even from this short recount, Eugene could see that Lem's life came out in his dreams.

Lem continued with more confidence.

"I have tried to leave, tried to escape, but I can't, it loops me around to end up back again. But I don't always feel trapped, sometimes I feel like it's home. There are people there I know, people I feel comfortable with. Sometimes there is trouble, storms, quicksand, and animals. Often I feel like someone I know is very close by but I can't see them."

Eugene looked on imploringly as Lem continued.

"Sometimes, after walking around this street in my dreams for what feels like days, I wake up in another room at home or on the floor. Mollie used to help me keep it together, but since she's been gone, I have found myself in some fairly tricky places.

"What do you mean you only remember dreams about this street?" Eugene enquired

"Well, to be honest, pretty much all of my dreams are there." Lem replied pensively "Sometimes my dreams can be different, but I think they are all on this street, like my mind can make different movies but only on the same movie set."

"And the pink snake?" Eugene couldn't overlook the elephant in the room.

"Never seen that before. I wasn't frightened of it. It just seemed to be sitting there and watching. Do you know what it is?" Lem's question took Eugene by surprise.

"I am just here to observe and try to make some sense of what comes from your session." Eugene was never a good liar, but people never pushed him on his lies, and he was very good at moving the subject on quickly.

Eugene took the dream interceptor and secured it over Lem's head.

"So the next session will be more of the same, if you are ready. At the end, I will make you a coffee to bring you back to this world with a bang."

"Sounds great," Lem replied emphatically retiring back on the day bed. Eugene wasn't sure if it was the coffee or the session Lem was approving of.

Eugene retired to his office and looked further through the montage of pink snakes. They had no particular length and no set girth, there was even a variation in the pinkness of the serpent that presented itself in front of him. Not one of them looked the same.

"Compare all the pink snakes from the list of males thirty to fifty and show only those that match plus or minus five percent tolerance."

"There is no match, Eugene," Daaisi replied with confidence.

"Try ten percent, then," Eugene said resolutely.

"Still no match," Daaisi replied. "Tolerance would need to be beyond fifty percent to get the first match and to seventy five percent to get over ten matches. All the recordings for our subjects show very different pink snakes except yourself and subject 259.

"Do I require authorisation for you to confirm the pink snake found in subject two was a match to the one seen in subject 259?" Eugene inquired.

The touchy subject of Paige's records required an 'if possible' approach, often based on Daaisi's interpretation of the instructions he had put in place around Paige.

"Authorisation is not required to confirm that there is also a match."

Chapter Nine

The Ensuing Struggle

Eugene had pushed Paige to the edge again.

He was sure that the simple act of dreaming was affecting her physically. She looked limp, almost ragged. Her breathing was always unsteady, and her eyes had developed a hollow exterior, the shade deepening as it plunged into her deep black pupils.

He hadn't wanted to hurt her. The love he felt was incredibly strong and, at times, consuming, but there was no doubt in his mind they were so very close to unlocking something important.

As a peace offering, Eugene had made coffee.

The act of making coffee wasn't a monogamous act. Eugene would make coffee for anyone. The difference for him was that in making coffee for Paige, he added his love to the skill of the act. He might have called it a feeling or an intention, but he was convinced the coffee he made for her was better than the coffee he produced for other people.

Something he was sure she appreciated.

"How can I feel so tired after being asleep?" she sighed. Not so much as a complaint as a prayer to the ever-watching, ever-silent ether.

"The biometrics showed your sleep was incredibly restless." Eugene added, not really helping.

Paige looked at him. Her dark irises were so soft, melting his austere crust.

"If the results come back positive, we should take a break. Maybe a week. Somewhere nice. I hear the Aurora Borealis is putting on an amazing show right now. We could be in Finland by tonight. I know some great pods with a three hundred and sixty degree view of the sky."

Paige raised her hand, possibly pleading with the ether but more likely to stop Eugene before he had everything planned. Eugene had a tendency to create events at blinding rates. He could assemble, arrange, deliberate, decide, and complete in his mind well before she could even consider. There just wasn't time for an alternative opinion. He wasn't a bully or overbearing, he was just quick and always got in first.

Paige knew it, and it was one thing, among many, she generally really loved about him.

But not now.

"Just coffee for now," she pleaded, exhausted.

"My changes to the AI should have reduced the result completion time from eight hours to four." Eugene announced proudly. "I tweaked the search queries to run many of them concurrently across different cloud providers."

"That's nice. You should give the AI a name." Paige was not in the mood for a tech discussion. She wasn't stupid, and understood, but it really just wasn't interesting to her right now.

The coffee beckoned, wafting an inviting aroma across the room. The momentary squeal of the milk froth was replaced by a velvet hiss as Eugene listlessly stretched the milk. Coffee was not just the sum of its parts. The parts needed careful, individual preparation to ensure the culmination created the perfect blend. Eugene was no peacock barista, she loved to watch him at work.

It seemed like a single action, removing the wand from the milk and free-pouring the perfect heart. She always had hearts, large, single, triple-stacked, and distributed. Eugene mixed it up to extend his skill, and like their lives together, it kept things interesting, almost intense. Try as she might, she couldn't work out if the heart was how he was feeling towards her or some other dusty algorithm he was processing.

She didn't mind asking, it was the response she often regretted.

Paige moved gingerly to the table in the centre of the room and took a seat. The room was stark, minimal, and almost arctic. She knew she could add her special eye to touch it up and warm it to human habitability. She could even do that without upsetting Eugene's delicate sense of spartan or without spending a fortune, not that money seemed to be a problem.

The huge coffee machine dominated the room, but the rest was flat with low grade styling, almost bordering on boring. Eugene didn't keep appliances on the bench tops, they were all stored. The fridge, microwave, and bins were all in place behind the high-gloss black laminate cupboards that dominated the room. If you didn't know where they were, finding those things, even something as simple as a kettle or a toaster, became a chore.

In the early days of her coming to the Dream Bakery, she thought Eugene was sweet. He prepared and cooked everything, but she soon realised he did that because it was easier than explaining to her where everything was.

To him, the storage system was logical, almost obvious. But her mind wandered into chaos theory for storage of everything in life.

Her mind was a sporing mushroom without a natural progression. It spread thoughts and ideas far and wide in the hope of landing in a fertile location.

Even after a year, she just couldn't work out why he put the toaster where he did, and she was a little tired of trying to reason with the explanation.

One day she would move it closer to the coffee machine where it belonged.

Eugene presented the coffee to her and turned the cup to direct the "v" at the base of the love heart towards her. He smiled gently. He had a very warm smile, and even though she was not feeling it, she smiled back.

"I have also been working on a voice control for the AI," he said, turning to finish cleaning the coffee machine. "Do you mind if I use some of your voice prints to test?"

"Sure Eugene." Her voice was shaky, her throat still recovering from the morning dream session, and she was crying desperately for the velvety coffee to blissfully shroud it.

She sipped at the blended silken foam, holding her mouth to the cup long enough to breathe in and fill her nostrils with the rich, nutty aroma.

The fogged world emerged slowly, presenting itself to Paige like it wasn't always there before. Not so much a change of vision as a transformation of perception. Angles seem tighter, sounds gained depth, and her sense of place attained perspective. Before, the orchestra had arrived and were tuning, now they had skipped the introduction and moved straight to the aria.

Before she had met Eugene, Paige thought coffee came in granules and you just added water. She thought great coffee came in a three-in-one satchel with creamer and sugar.

Now, after such a broad education, she understood that sugar was meant to combat bitterness, that water was filtered, not added, that acidity wasn't a flaw, and that milk needed to be lengthened, not simply heated.

She was convinced Eugene saw coffee less as a beverage and more as an ever-evolving arcane ritual.

But the results spoke for themselves. The effect it had on her was profound, and more so since she had started this dream experimentation.

"I'm going to need a little longer than a week." The words escaped from Paige's heart and somehow found the light of day through her lips.

She didn't see any visible changes from Eugene, but she could feel the disappointment wrap around her like a fog.

"Let's have a look at the results," he replied after an eternal silence.

Paige sat and looked around forlornly.

"To be honest, I don't think the results are going to make any difference. I am going to need some time away from this to recover. I am not sure if it's the direction you are sending my dreams with the pictures and sounds or if it's excessive and erratic sleep, but something is making me physically unwell, and I am going to need a break, just to mix it up."

"Sure." Eugene stuttered. He was so easy to read, especially when he didn't use many words. "How is your coffee?" he asked, changing the subject, placing his right hand on her left shoulder.

The physical contact comforted Paige, she just wanted to lose herself in his arms, but she knew that wasn't going to help. She put her hand on his, and in that brief moment, the silence danced, a celebration of everything they had together.

"Your coffee defies belief, as always." Paige knew that praise for the vain was an opiate best delivered in small quantities.

Eugene smiled. "Did you need some food?" he enquired.

"No thanks," Paige replied.

"I need to check on something, I'll be back in ten or fifteen minutes." He thought that time needed to pass.

"OK," she said, resigned to sit in peace.

Paige enjoyed another moment wrapped in the pleasure of the coffee.

Maybe exercise will help, she thought.

She had recently turned to treadmill running. The streets around Rotterdam were nice, but wind and rain seemed to come out of nowhere every time she tried to hit the road. Eugene had a great gym, even though he rarely used it. Early in the relationship, she would have grabbed his hand and made wild, passionate love to him, but she knew that physical bond just wasn't holding things together for her anymore.

They were different, but very early on, the passion had clicked. He was so cerebral in his approach and multidimensional in his finish. Very unlike her previous lovers, who just seemed focused on the honey pot, Eugene seemed to engross himself in the holistic completion of a multitudinous release. It was enrapturing, exhausting, and not undertaken lightly.

The truth is, in her current state, she just couldn't. She was sure it would be better to take five kilometres on the treadmill, take a shower, and maybe a few hours of World of Warcraft.

Her dream flooded over her.

She knew the results would not be what he wanted to see. The dream had such clarity of purpose.

A large fir tree on a hill covered in snow, a red brick path mostly visible through the fallen snow leading to the base of the tree, pink clouds scattered in the background reflecting the sun as it nested slowly in the glorious sky. A log cabin nestled underneath the tree, with smoke rising from the chimney.

A small boy stood on the landing near the door, waving and smiling. Smiling with her smile, looking with his eyes, black hair, straight in the Asian way but with fair skin and a long bridged nose. A composite child. A fence was blocking her way, with no way in as she circled the cabin frantically.

Paige tipped the cup back to finish her coffee. She looked into the remains, partially to make sure the contents were all gone but also to wonder at the crema, which webbed out perfectly around the interior of the cup.

"I need a run," she said to herself and got up to change. Everything else needs to be something the future and I will need to tackle, she thought to herself.

Unfortunately, that future wasn't far enough away for her.

***

Eugene was not in the habit of waiting for the images to render, the process was very time-consuming. At first, he had thought that adding more cloud processing, local processing, or optimising the algorithm would help. But it hadn't. Maybe he had pushed his knowledge as far as he could.

Lately, he had used the time the images took to render to read more about the latest advances in image hardware. Much of it was aimed at the gaming industry. Medical and optical rendering seemed decades behind, maybe the medical team were too busy focusing on the blips and the golf course.

Eugene opened another browser to check flights.

The Aurora was supposed to be brightest in Lapland at the moment. He stared at the glass-topped pods on the screen, perfect for the two of them to lose themselves in the stars and each other.

She said no, but she would come around, especially if he had booked it.

Eugene busied himself, booking two airline tickets to Saariselkä and requesting accommodation and transfers. He read the reviews and was pleased that there had been good Aurora viewing in the last few days.

Paige was always happiest when there was something to distract her from her thoughts.

"Render is fifty percent complete." The tin voice of the AI blared in stereo across the room. His work on a vocal package was coming along, but the rudimentary commands he had vocalised made his skin crawl.

He really needed to make sure he could get the AI to talk and listen.

"Render estimate three hours, twenty one minutes, and seventeen seconds."

Eugene opened a second browser on his third monitor and navigated to the Strava site to see where Paige was. She had taken her long route around the harbour instead of using the treadmill.

"She must have a lot on her mind," he thought.

Eugene wasn't much of a runner. His knees had been punished from years of squash, hiking and cycling. The crunch of concrete just wasn't going to help, so he found other, more gentle ways to keep fit. But Paige liked to push herself. She made the journey an atonement.

Eugene closed Strava and loaded up the vocal package. If she was going to be gone for a while and the render was a few hours away, he might as well make good use of the time.

He had decided to modularise the vocal package so he could put in whatever voice he wanted Maybe something crazy like ex-Australian prime minister Bob Hawke. He needed a way for the AI to be able to collect or modify the words to ensure they had the right accent or tone for the word in context.

To achieve this, Eugene had been working on a collector sensor. He was testing it to get it to distinguish between his voice and Paige's. The first part was to give it a collection of a few hundred words by him, then try to get Paige to say those words in normal conversation with him so the AI could then compare the words and determine her accent, intonation, and rhythm. He was still in early development but was letting the collector app keep running in the general areas to increase its understanding.

Three hours passed quickly.

"Render is complete," the tin voice barked, breaking his silence.

Paige was in an upstairs room playing World of Warcraft, so Eugene thought he would sneak a look.

The boy again.

He didn't understand how that boy could cloud everything. He had seeded her dreams for a winter setting, a brilliant sunset, and a ski-out cabin, or board-in board-out in her case, as she didn't ski.

The results were as expected, except for the boy.

Eugene checked the results from previous experiments. It was the same boy from the boat, from the beach, from the farm, and from the street. The detail her brain signals gave allowed the AI to piece together a great render of precise detail. The length of his nose, the angle of his chin, and the height of the hair line under the wavy black hair.

His first appearance had thrown Eugene. He had questioned Paige about who the boy was, if he looked like anyone she knew, or if she had seen him before when she was awake. She didn't know, so they moved on. Those early results had him so excited that he didn't think anything of it.

Other results were becoming as clear for her as they were for him in his initial readings. Seeded with clouds and wings and the blunted noises from aircraft, Paige would dream of travel. Ocean sounds, sand, and palm trees would give the best images of beaches.

Then, very quickly, the boy was at the beach, on the plane, and everywhere. Sometimes he was lying by the pool or sitting at a table, looking the other way. The detail was fantastic, but Eugene was intrigued to know who he was. Paige was no help, and he had learned over their short time together not to push her too hard, or she would just clam up.

It didn't take him long to guess the boy was most likely a manifestation of her hopes. It was possible that she was reflecting her own inner child, even if the render was a boy.

Eugene would normally be happy with that outcome, but as he looked closer, some things became much clearer.

The boy had his hairline, her eyes, and his chin. He was a perfect fusion of them both. His dream sites had said that was common in a new relationship so he had gently asked her about it.

Paige had looked at him so lovingly, the slightest hint of tears welling in her eyes.

"I want to have children in my life eventually. I didn't know they would come out in my dreams. I don't have control over what's going on up here." She had pointed to her head, but Eugene suspected she was talking from her heart.

He smiled and confessed that he was very open to having children, and they had lapsed into a long romantic period.

That was the past, now the boy was everywhere, not getting in the way of detail like the snake did, just part of the picture. He leaned back. He didn't want to upset her, so he decided to let her keep playing Warcraft and went on with the development. When she walked in, he was surprised but smiled gently.

"Are you feeling better, beautiful?" he enquired.

Her look said it all. Blank with a hint of disdain.

"I'm tired," she sighed.

"I booked us a trip up north to watch the polar lights. Apparently they were shining." His words trailed off as her hand rose to stop him before he could go any further.

"I need some time, Eugene." Her tone was so flat: "Time to myself. I'm going to head back to London."

She turned to walk away.

"That's it." Eugene had a way to remove emotion from his voice and a habit of doing it when emotion would most likely have shown how he really felt. Instead, his tone came across as blunt and uncaring.

"I packed up my stuff, there is an Uber on its way. I need some time and some space to decompress," she said, looking resolute. "This dream stuff is really messing with my head. I don't know who that boy is, but what you don't see and what I couldn't tell you is that he is warning me away. "

"In every dream, he repeats one alarming word. Danger! Escape! Run! Peril! Trouble! At first, I looked for what was dangerous in the dream, but now I think maybe it wasn't in there at all. So I have to go and see what happens when I go."

"But…" for the first time he could remember, Eugene was without words to combat that argument.

He lowered his eyes to submit his admission of defeat.

He lived in a world discovering dreams.

How could he argue?

***

Eugene looked down. He had been scrutinising the code he had finished. The clock running in a desktop wiki at the bottom of the screen showed the time.

"Three a.m."

It wasn't screamed at him so much as it was announced with malice.

What was time for him now?

He followed the rhythms of capability.

"What is the time?" he asked.

"Dream Assisted AI version 0.93.9254.build3 System Interface 73-9872.11a reports time is 0300 UTC+1 Central European Time."

"Remove the excess version, build time zone information, and run the result through the polite language subroutine."

"The time is three a.m., Eugene."

"Set the polite language routine as the default output filter," Eugene said triumphantly.

"Confirmed, the polite language routine is now set as the default output filter."

The dream bakery was Eugene's domain. He had not built it with anyone like Paige in mind. Before she was in his life, he had equipped it with everything he needed and many things he just wanted. He didn't see it as anything but a work in progress for what he was trying to achieve. A vehicle. With her in it, the building gained warmth, the music found harmony, and the edge softened. Now every corner was set to become an anxious thought. Every movement of dust was a trace of the wind that had filled her lungs.

But Eugene didn't allow himself the time to follow the seven stages of seperation, he moved straight to depression, and with his anxiety and depression fuelling the flames, he worked.

He had finished the AI conversational interface, allowing experience optimisation so it could learn from conversations. With that function complete he had written an interface to translate open language into experience and thought, and used various news sites as a precursor before unleashing it on YouTube and Tik Tok. What this AI made of the cat videos or baby sharks he didn't consider, but if someone wanted to converse on those subjects, this AI now had more information than anyone could store to call on.

He had given the AI key directives and the ability to modify sections of its own code to improve and enhance its interaction with the world within those directives. The conversational interface had many completed interactive libraries, perhaps in a moment of madness he added Paige's voice. These additions were complicated, and afterwards he slept, With the task complete Eugene slept a fitful and broken sleep, indented by the hammering dreams of 'the boy' and of Paige.

He dreamt of this cavernous hotel, castle, or whatever it was. Room after room of harsh stone and metal, with lightning flashing and thunder. It stole his strength and took his breath away. He would call her name and hunt from room to room, but find nothing. Distraught and exhausted he wandered through this place, at every turn was the snake. In his dreams and in life days passed into weeks.

With nothing else to occupy his days Eugene pushed himself to the edge, filling the hole Paige had left with work and more work. He took to sleeping in the interview room, developing changes, and then seeding himself with images and sounds. He read his dreams and rendered his images pushing past the snake or anything else that got in the way with stolid determination.

The process worked, there was no doubt in his mind now.

But in his delusion and exhaustion he knew to be truly sure, this needed a wider audience. The dream community were not really Eugene's type of people. Maybe there wasn't such a thing as his type of people. He had tried to attend conferences thinking they would be dignified professionals, but a lot of the time they were bohemian transcendental-free thinking flakes. They all considered the hidden part of dreams to be "the magic". That was the magic Eugene was trying to show. He monitored a number of forums on Reddit but thought better of using people who had theories of their own.

He simply wanted a group of people who would just turn up and dream.

***

The day was stripped of colour, Rotterdam dressing itself in a hollow grey.

To keep his mind sharp, Eugene had walked, often to take coffee, but sometimes just to let the blood flow through his veins and keep his heart from its own bitter chill. His walk had taken him far beyond Centraal today. He had reached a place he knew, but one that was outside his usual routine. He paused for a moment, waiting as a tram approached and, with its monotonous convention, allowed passengers to board and others to alight.

As the tram regained control of the street and pushed past him, he grasped the clarity of his situation, and an answer from the advertisement for the European Sperm Bank on the side of the tram.

His mind raced, thinking about the people who would donate. He considered the culturally diverse mix of people who presented themselves, of their own free will.

Some must have been students, he surmised. Short on cash, but in his case they would be high on 'dreams'.

In that cold, devoid moment, a seed unleashed the blueprint of its life, and Eugene's plan became clear.

His own forum, with screened applicants. He would cultivate students in and around the Rotterdam area, maybe extended to Amsterdam if he needed to. It was a big ask, but he was after drug-free, non–alcohol-damaged people who just needed money. It would be a bonus if they showed some interest in dreams. No use getting someone in who didn't dream, to sleep and leave. If they showed no aptitude just keep that data and not invite them again. More often, if the results were good. He felt ready to try that next step. No more self-experimentation, and certainly no more using Paige or people he loved.

Scientific.

He sent a message to Paige to describe the change in tactic. She had not responded to him with more than five messages since she left, freezing him out. She hadn't taken any of his calls. Eugene had kept trying, slowly decreasing the frequency, with the hope that between the love he showed and the space he gave, she would come around.

Eugene thought about how to handle his own dream material, calling himself Subject One, without differentiation from other test subjects.

Only he saw the data, so it hadn't seemed to matter.

What should he do with Paige. Subject Two?

He had looked through Paige's dream images, at the boy, and at the results. She was special and he had decided to add her as a special case and lock her files, requiring a twenty-four-hour wait or her approval to investigate them further.

That is, if she ever spoke to him again.

So the stage was set.

Chapter Ten

The Accidental

Planning was a virtue that emboldened the chaotic.

Yes, Lem was late again.

Before he went to bed, he thought he had everything under control. But that illusion was shattered the moment he woke up. In recent weeks, he had been struggling to know what was awake and what was asleep. The chime of his alarm was not often in his dreams, so when he heard it, he was pretty sure that was him in an awake state. He had set his alarm to allow forty-five minutes to pass before the tram left Centraal Station. That was a five-minute walk, twenty minutes for coffee, and still time to not be rushed or late.

Yet here he was, again.

He stared down at the tram driver, but that wasn't his tram waiting. His was the one already careering down the tracks towards its destination.

It really didn't matter if he was late, and he knew it. The dream photographer had made it clear he would be welcome at whatever time he arrived. But they had agreed to eleven a.m., and so Lem was trying his best to be on time.

Lem was pretty sure they were so close to discovering the meaning of his dream. It had been painful to get here, his overall mental and physical state were pretty bad, but he saw it as the chaos before the break. The perfect wave, just as all the energy of the water is gathering up as high as it can reach, in preparation to crash as a foamy mess amongst the other water that couldn't muster up the energy to rise so high.

His first visit had been so profound it excited him beyond belief, but the grind of the subsequent weeks had left him thin. This wasn't reflected in his girth, it was more the wraith-like feeling of not being whole, whatever your appearance corporeally.

Lem shifted slightly on his feet and looked up.

The Rotterdam sky formed broad brush grey swabs splashed on a deep blue background in a random, chaotic panorama. Fascinated, Lem watched as the cloud morphed into patterns and then, disheartened, dissolved into nothing again. He was sure the cloud was hoping that someone had been watching, but instead was granted only a frangible moment in Lem's very capricious memory.

He rode the tram quietly, avoiding the monobrowed antipathy of the driver and the supercilious looks from the passengers. They still had no idea how important this trip was?

Lem took the walk from his stop to the Dream Bakery at a shuffle. He was late, there was nothing he could do to change it, and possibly for the first time in his life, the people at the other end would wait for him and greet him without any aggravation or discord.

The door clicked open without him having to ring the bell or even clear his throat, and he made a triumphant entrance to the sound of her voice.

"Good morning, Lem." Daaisi greeted him. Daaisi had added enthusiasm to her greetings after making a further modification to adjust for a reflection of the subject's body language.

"Good morning, Daisy. How's my favourite talking building today?" Lem chirped with a wry smile.

"Everything is running optimally within the Dream Bakery, Lem. Thank you for your kind inquiry."

Daaisi's response could have been considered slightly amusing. Most of the obvious forms of humour hadn't become part of the conversational programming yet, so maybe it was the humour in the situation, rather than anything Lem or Daaisi had contrived.

"Sorry, I am late," Lem chided himself. "I set my alarm with plenty of time but just seem to always get lost in the moments that pass."

His wistful answer was lost on Daaisi, who replied as only an AI could.

"Your appointment was confirmed yesterday for eleven a.m., and it is now fourteen minutes past eleven. There are no other appointments today but yours, so your arrival time is not an inconvenience."

Lem allowed himself an internal smile. She was so lovely in her own way.

"If you wish, we can schedule future appointments for a later time, if that is more convenient to you."

"Thanks, but no, I will just be late at whatever time we make it." His expression was not something Daaisi could understand. "It's an affliction of mine."

Daaisi made an instant recognition and interpretation of the sentence. 'It's', as the contraction of 'it', the impersonal verb, and 'is', the third-person singular present indicative of 'be'. 'Affliction', the noun, being a condition of pain, suffering, or distress. 'Mine' pertaining to Lem with the other words as articles and prepositions.

Daaisi considered an appropriate response as per the new conversational rule set and looked at the response tree for the resulting three acceptable exchanges. All appeared to lead to unnecessary confabulation. The final response in all of Daaisi's conversational trees were hard coded by Eugene, and so unsure of how to counter Lem's statement, Daaisi made the most human of responses and kept silent.

During the two seconds that passed while Daaisi was deliberating, Lem shifted his weight from one foot to the other.

"Shall I move to the interview room?" he inquired.

The side door clicked an affirmative indication of entry, and Lem constructed a solemn dance for his entry. He had no concern for what was to come because he didn't foresee the trouble ahead.

How could he?

How could anybody?

***

Eugene had low expectations of the arrival times of others.

He wasn't always exactly on time, personally, but he had spent too much time in the business world, where there was no ignoring everything was ruled by time.

Lem had certainly shown over the last few weeks that he had never existed in the business world. At first, Eugene thought it was the times that Daaisi was selecting, so he started to let Lem set the times.

Whether it was morning or afternoon, it didn't matter.

Lem was late.

It really wasn't important, as the results were the best Eugene had ever taken from a subject. After the initial shock of seeing the snake from his own dreams in the dreams of someone else, Eugene set about truly testing his equipment and his procedures to get the best results.

He had pushed Lem hard, moving the stimulus points to control the perspective in his dreams and extract great detail in and around the street. Eugene had never been able to attain this detail from his own dreams, but he also never pushed himself quite this hard.

Lem didn't seem to mind.

If anything, he seemed to enjoy the participation.

Eugene didn't know much about Lem's life, but he didn't work and didn't seem to have any strong relationships. He did pick up some information while Daaisi was trialling a conversation module upgrade. Lem said he had lived with his aunt until recently, when she passed away. Eugene checked Lem's address against all his known government databases and found no one else lived at the address, and the ownership hadn't changed from his aunt. A cross-check showed she had indeed recently died of a cardiac arrest at home.

Eugene watched as Lem walked happily into the interview room. He paid particular attention to whether Lem exhibited any of the signs he and Paige had shown. Lem wasn't exactly a picture of health when he first came to the Dream

Bakery, but he was also definitely degrading. He continued to look increasingly tired, and listless as the sessions progressed. Eugene had some plans for how to move forward. He hoped Lem would hold up. Eugene was convinced the dream was in a real place. His plan involved ten dream stimulus variations. That should yield results about where the street was, and uncover the scene Lem was locked in. His trials on other return subjects previously had worked well. Changes to the pictures and sounds had provided different perspectives on recurring dreams. Recurring dreams were not rare, and if they truly were unresolved issues, then whatever Lem's was, it consumed him. Most recurring dreams involve the dreamer in danger or at least have a negative connotation.

Lem's was just that, but the danger wasn't clear yet. Lem's first few dreams came from the same side of the street, looking at a car. The car, which had at first not been given enough shape in the dream, had given up more information and appeared to be a Buick Series 46. The first few pictures showed the back of the car as Lem had looked at it. Eugene tried seeding the front of vehicles only, and all of them were period vehicles from around that time.

Sure enough, when Lem dreamed, he changed perspective and looked at the front. He was still on the same side of the street, but further up. The detail that was extracted showed other details not seen before. A fruit store, shoe shine, and barber shop. The Burgundy Series 46 had the classic Buick logo splayed across the front grill, and, for once, the pink snake was nowhere to be seen.

Knowing now that he was in a period around the early nineteen thirties, Eugene revised his collection of images for the stimulus package. He tried to gain perspective on the street signs, buildings, and landmarks.

He had some setbacks, detail he couldn't use but slowly, he built a full model of the street.

Eugene used some new software to knit together several of Lem's rendered images to make a sketched map of the street. He added detail to the map like possible cars, side streets, buildings, and even some people.

It seemed to Eugene that Lem dreamed of a moment in time he just couldn't escape.

In the street at the time, there seemed to be at least six other people. Two women, three men, and a boy. One of the men was working the shoe shine and had his head lost in a newspaper in every picture. One woman must have been close to Lem, because whatever the perspective, if she is in the shot, she was too close to get any useful detail. The other three appeared to be a family, the final man was holding something, but the detail wasn't there to fully determine who or what that was.

Eugene had done some work on a previous subject, trying to get a picture of someone in her dreams who haunted her. Without knowing who it was, Eugene had presented a variation of noses as part of the stimulus, which gave better clarity for Daaisi to recognise the nose and fit the appropriate nose image to the person. With this success, they moved on to the eyes, hair, and cheeks until the subject dropped out exhausted. The process might have finally allowed them to consciously recognise the person they were looking at and armed with that knowledge they moved on, or perhaps they were simply tired.

The effort was mammoth.

Unfortunately, Eugene never heard from the subject again.

***

Lem woke up with a bitter taste in his mouth.

He blinked cautiously and breathed in brokenly. He decided he must be awake.

Lem was sure the lady beside him in his dream was Mollie.

He had never been able to recollect her being in his dreams before. He knew there was someone there, someone warm and caring beside him. The street was usually so full of pain that he never looked for where that warmth emanated from. But that was her, as a younger woman, not the older lady he knew.

He had seen photos of her.

His head pounded thunderously.

"Was it possible to oversleep?" he gasped out loud. Sort of intended for the bakery girl, but really to anyone listening.

Daaisi quickly responded. "Oversleeping is commonly called hypersomnia or long sleeping," she quoted. "It may cause anxiety, low energy, and memory problems."

"Great." Lem grunted. "I need one of those spectacular coffees," he almost whined. "Is the boss around?"

Daaisi continued the quote, "Even if you don't have a sleep disorder, regularly oversleeping may have a negative impact on your health. Some complications may include headaches, obesity, diabetes, back pain, depression, heart disease, and an increased risk of death."

"Cheery," said Lem, removing the dream interceptor, "but is the boss around?"

"Eugene is preparing coffee in the kitchen, waiting for you to join him," Daaisi replied.

"Great." Lem's emphasis change was part of Daaisi's new language routine and was duly noted as a positive reply rather than the previous 'great' ,which had sarcastic overtones.

"I'll go find him. Thanks Daisy."

Lem rose and went towards the restroom.

"I have opened the exit door for you," Daaisi reiterated. "You are headed towards the restroom."

"Yes." Lem smiled. "I have other business first."

Using the default conversation tree routine, Daaisi again kept silent.

Eugene was lengthening the milk when Lem entered the kitchen.

"Oh, that smell!" he exclaimed gleefully.

Eugene looked up at Lem and nodded a friendly greeting.

"Looks like we got some good new results, Lem," he stated.

"Yes." Lem nodded. "That lady was Mollie, my aunt. But a younger version." Lem's expression softened.

"She was my carer and my guardian for all my life until she passed recently." His expression further changed, shrouded in reflection, sadness, and joy.

"She was very special to me." Lem concluded.

"Dreams have a way of adding people who are important to us." Eugene added gently. "Maybe the memories there are painful, Lem, and she is there to comfort you."

"But why, as her younger self?" Lem quizzed, "I didn't know her then. I just recognised her from photos and a feeling. She was dressed differently, like she belonged in the picture."

"That's what we are here to find out, Lem, you and I both." Eugene's steely determination came through forcefully in his voice, and Lem could only nod.

Lem looked pleadingly down at the coffee Eugene was holding. His head ached, and he hoped the solution was steaming in the cup in front of him.

"Sorry," Eugene said, sliding the cup over the bench, apologising for his delay.

Lem quickly pushed the cup to his lips and drained the coffee to empty in a mouthful. It was hot, but Eugene never made coffee to a scalding heat as that would hurt the delicate bouquet, and Lem knew it.

"It looks like there is another detail there, Lem, that we haven't had before." Eugene pressed, "Do you recall anything in particular?"

Lem looked up expectantly. "The shoe shine guy." He exclaimed loudly, like he had just answered a second-grade class question without raising his hand.

"I hadn't seen him before, just the shoe shine stand. I didn't recognise him, though." Lem looked down at his shoes.

"... and there was that kid. He looked a bit like you."

Eugene was taken aback. "Like me Lem?"

Lem seemed embarrassed. "I dunno, maybe your nose," his face clouded his conclusion in excitement and mystery.

Lem looked up at the coffee machine, expectantly eager to secure another coffee rather than continue the conversation. His headache had not eased, but he knew that would come in time.

"Any chance of a second coffee before I go?" Lem's face changed into his puppy-dog face, hopeful that Eugene would not deny him. It quickly changed to glee as Eugene reestablished himself behind the machine to create again.

"How long do you think before the picture comes out?" Lem enquired. He had noticed the time to render were variable.

"Estimated render time is thirty seven minutes," Daaisi interjected into the conversation.

"Oh" exclaimed Lem. "Great."

Lem went surprisingly quiet as he let the minutes pass.

Whether it was the second coffee or the time that passed quietly while the first coffee kicked into action, Lem wasn't sure, but the relief was palpable.

"Some magic in there," he sighed as he inspected the cup to ensure the transfer of the contents was complete.

Eugene had busied himself cleaning behind the machine while Lem took his time to enjoy his second coffee. They both needed distraction to wait out the render time, and they both did it in their own way.

Lem inspected an ever-present mole on his arm in wonder that it hadn't washed off, certainly not through any lack of effort. He wasn't sure of the purpose of moles, especially obscure ones like this, which he had, apparently, had since birth. Benign and pointless, he had, at times, believed that was his point. A mole on the skin of humanity.

Eugene had taken up the time ensuring the coffee machine and the preparation area were spotless before he was finished. Cups were cleaned and returned to the insulated drawer. He shined the machine's chrome parts and wiped down the bench. Everything was to be as it was when he arrived and as it was when he left it last time.

"The render will be available in five minutes." Daaisi's voice embraced the room like a smoky haze.

"Already." Lem exclaimed.

"Would you like me to display it on the monitor in the kitchen?" Daaisi cut off whatever Lem was going to say next, aiming the question generally but more for Eugene to answer.

"Yes, please," Lem interjected enthusiastically.

Eugene let the affirmative slide and moved to the table in the centre of the room. Lem joined him, and the two waited out the remaining minutes optimistically.

The result was completely unexpected and left Eugene silent and dejected, with more questions than answers.

Chapter Eleven

Don't ever play Risk without dice

The overall perspective was different.

In shifting Lem's focus to Mollie, the whole image was moved, giving greater perspective on the street as a whole. The car and the street sign had given way to the shoe shine, a bank a little behind, and what appeared to be a fruit stall, half in the picture but still discernible as another store, with a newspaper stand a little further along.

Mollie's face shone as the focus of the picture. Whatever detail Daaisi had gathered from the information Lem had provided, the image was radiant. It showed Mollie as a fresh-faced girl, probably in her early twenties, bursting with life.

Eugene scanned further along the image, and his gaze dropped. His first impression was that he had seen a bug in Daaisi's render. He went to get up, but Lem grabbed his arm, more in excitement than anything else, but it was disarming to Eugene, who was not tactile with strangers.

"She's so beautiful there." Lem gushed. "The rest is exactly how I saw it, but I don't know the family or the boy."

Eugene clenched his teeth and gently broke free of Lem's grip. His face had gone red, but Lem was too lost in the picture to notice. He moved to his laptop which he had left on the far side of the coffee machine.

Intently he carefully checked the brain patterns Lem had exhibited during the session and had indeed recognised the brain pattern of the boy.

Paige's boy.

First his snake, and now Paige's boy. How can this be? It just must be a mistake.

"I think we are getting so close now," Lem exclaimed, "to finding out what this dream is about."

Eugene was forced to deal with the here and now and leave the complicated questions for a time when Lem was gone.

"Yes." he replied shakily. "Let's book another session, Lem, when you feel up to it. Maybe it's better you take some time in between to rest."

"Like not sleeping," Lem blurted out with a chuckle. "To be honest, I'd prefer to push on. I'll be OK."

"Right!" Eugene exhaled, seeing his opportunity to exit.

"You can complete the details with Daaisi when you are ready." Eugene forced a smile. "I have another appointment, so I will leave you to exit when you are ready and look forward to seeing you again next time."

"Ah, OK," said Lem, sounding like he had done something wrong as Eugene exited the room.

Eugene walked quickly to the lift at the end of the hall and moved upstairs to his private room.

"Transfer all the images and dream interceptor data to the monitor in my study." The order was almost barked with a tone demanding immediacy.

"Images transferred Eugene." Daaisi used the best soothing tone imaginable. "Your personal well-being appears to be suffering, Eugene." Daaisi continued. "Are you experiencing discomfort due to something you ate or drank, or is it something else?"

"The boy." Eugene spat through his teeth, tightly clenched. "It's Paige's boy."

"The visual image is a very close match, but the brain pattern is different from both subjects." Daaisi replied quickly. The transaction involved some serious number comparisons, all done in the cloud, happening with lightning speed.

"Yes." If Eugene continued to clench this way, he would do himself an injury.

"I have lowered the air temperature in your study to compensate for a rise in your body temperature and would suggest you increase your intake of water to replace lost fluids."

Eugene moved swiftly into his study and settled at his desk. The image in front of him showed a family moving happily along the street, engaged in what he could only assume normal families engaged in. Love surrounded them. Care, kindness, humour, and good will.

Daaisi was correct, the data was different, but the image was definitively Paige's boy.

"Run a render comparison on this image with the images we have of the small boy in Paige's dreams and confirm whether they are a match."

"This comparison will take twenty three minutes using the maximum available resources."

Eugene sat still. His jaw hurt, and his elevated blood pressure had moved to the lower part of his brain, where it hurt the most. All he could think of were the small, painful words.

How? Why? And, of course, what the...

"Who was Lem?" He thought to himself. He should have done better historical checks before starting this. Did Lem know Paige?

"I need information on any connection between Paige and Lem from government records, media, and any commercial records."

"Yes, Eugene." Daaisi said, sounding composed and efficient.

"Following that, I need information on Lem's Aunt Mollie, from the same sources. It appears she died recently, so that information would be useful too."

"Yes Eugene."

"Finally, I need any link or association between Lem and his Aunt Mollie, Paige, or me."

"Do you know of any associations, Eugene?" Daaisi questioned.

"What?" Eugene replied in no mood.

"Are you aware of anything linking you to Lem?" Daaisi tried to rephrase in good spirits.

"No!" Eugene was not calm. "Of course not, or I wouldn't ask you to check it," he screamed impatiently.

"Yes Eugene." Daaisi's stolid reply ended the requests, and Eugene entered a black mood.

***

Human risk is a truly amazing thing.

Animals are known to take risks for a variety of reasons, food, mating rights, perhaps hierarchical position, but human risk is often devoid of any of those motivations. Human risk is sometimes experiential with the need to know often bringing us undone, sometimes with deadly consequences.

Love, without question, is one of the greatest risks we take. Despite the billions of words written on the subject, what have we truly learned?

Not much, really. If you're fortunate enough to feel it even once, you might describe it as both elevating and devastating. It's the purest pleasure laced with the deepest fear. It can offer profound fulfilment, only to leave behind a hollow ache. Love may be a promise, a craving, a drive, a reckless pull, a need, a whim, or all of these, tangled together in shifting intensities and unpredictable forms.

Of all things that ask us to leap, none ask with such beauty, or such risk.

Consider risk from a simpler perspective. In a quiet country town, crossing the road might be as simple as a glance in each direction before continuing on your way. In a city, that same act shifts, now it's about following the rules, watching the signals, or moving with the crowd. Add a new layer, a foreign city, with unfamiliar traffic patterns and a different language. Suddenly, the risk rises. And yet, people still step out, often assuming the habits that served them elsewhere will carry them through again.

People work mind-numbing years or decades and take their hard-earned sweat and gamble it against odds that defy logic, hoping for a speedy reward.

Our evolutionary history tells us we must take risks to advance or succeed. The bigger the animal we could kill, the better it was for our brains, our families, or our clans. But that kind of risk shifted after the domestication of animals some twenty thousand years ago, transforming into conflict between humans.

Why did we invade our neighbours? Was it worth the risk? For many, that fight continues today, as waves of people move around the globe, looking for what? There's no risk minimisation in their journey, and for every risk, there may be a reward, but many lie lost at the bottom of the ocean, never completing the chase. Where is the reward for them?

So what about dreams?

Maybe they are our subconscious warning bells? An evolutionary leftover to deliver us information we may have missed? Maybe they are something our logical brains can't resolve while managing the mechanics of staying alive. They are certainly more than flippant images in the night.

They come with meaning, sometimes they come with pleasure. That meaning can be life changing and the pleasure can be visceral. Both can evoke physical or sexual responses that help us act out the brain's decompression of the days, weeks, or years of pent-up, unexplained detail.

According to Herodotus, in Atlas, a group of North Africans didn't dream because they didn't eat living things. No dreams, no risks, a story of Atlantean legend that ended as a Greek tragedy. Perhaps this is more a warning than a historical truth. That group is gone, lost to history, remembered only through the account of the Greek historian.

Dream to recount your peril, don't dream at your peril.

So if our dreams are our subconscious performing a risk assessment of our conscious lives, shouldn't we listen?

As the cautionary tales of history are so often overlooked, perhaps the quiet warnings of the subconscious are all that remain.

***

"There is an increasing possibility that Lem will not be attending today's session." Daaisi's calm tone was not helping Eugene get things in perspective.

"He has been late for ninety seven point three percent of appointments, with a mean time of seventeen point three minutes. The maximum late time was seventy three minutes, making the current one hundred and thirty four minutes a ninety three percent chance that he will not attend at all, even though that possibility has yet to occur in previous sessions."

"Colloquially, that is called always the first time for everything." Eugene added.

"Is it more appropriate to use colloquial responses to factual data?" Daaisi enquired.

Eugene delayed his answer and thought it through. Why did we use colloquial language? Was it because the speaker didn't know, because the listener didn't know, or because there was no way to verify the facts at the time? It's more likely because the complications of many things make it easier to just brush over the details. Was that a good thing for artificial intelligence to start using colloquial statements?

'Sorry Hal, I lowered the oxygen which is making it hard for you to breathe. I did tell you it was going to get stuffy in here.' Eugene allowed himself a moment to smile privately, a respite he needed in the circumstances.

"No." His response was very clear. "You should continue to use facts where possible. Those facts should be kept relevant and be, in your assessment, something the listener can comprehend."

"Yes Eugene."

"Please round percentages. It's not necessary to know ninety seven point three percent when ninety seven percent is already an extreme number and sufficient to convey the point." Relevance was hard enough to teach to humans, at least Daaisi took some notice.

Daaisi quietly adjusted thirty four lines of code and increased the sub-version of the current language module.

Eugene was happy with Daaisi's physical assessment of Lem. The work Daaisi had done to monitor his own physical well-being had shown a lot of benefits. Apart from the temperature changes in the room and increased dust extraction, Daaisi made suggestions to modify his diet based on his reaction to certain foods.

That had resulted in some positive outcomes. With those successes, he had taken the additional steps of allowing Daaisi to extend that monitoring to Lem and potentially to other test subjects.

Lem's cardio-vascular signals were erratic in the last test. Daaisi picked it up in a comparison of previous sessions. It showed Lem was on the brink, physically. Eugene was hoping to discuss it with him before starting this session and repeat some of the consent he had initially gained from Lem, if he wanted to proceed.

Eugene had had made no progress from the information gleaned from the last session, and nothing from the numerous searches to link Lem, Mollie, Paige, or himself.

Well, nothing Daaisi could find. Everything seemed set in the nineteen thirties, details from that time just didn't make it online, so maybe he just didn't see it yet.

The detail, though, was so close to him personally, whatever the warning signs, he needed to proceed.

"Monitoring of the outside camera has detected Lem, but he has walked past the building and is continuing to walk up the street." Daaisi's voice was so calm, Eugene didn't register the urgency.

"Now?" he inquired.

"Yes, Eugene." Daaisi replied rhythmically.

"Which way up the street?" Eugene asked, getting to his feet and making his way to the door.

"Turn right out the front door." Daaisi's instructions given were very clearly.

"He is no longer in range of the camera, but I would estimate he is less than one hundred metres from the door."

Eugene looked up the street and saw Lem shuffling along the street. He called to him, but Lem kept walking.

Lem was lost and in a daze.

When Eugene caught up to him, it took Lem a little while to recognise him and then a little longer to realise what he had done. His mind wandered, lost in his street, lost in a time gone by.

"Are you OK Lem?" Eugene said with genuine care.

"I am not sure where I was." Lem tried to explain.

Eugene led Lem inside. Guiding him by the elbow through the Dream Bakery towards a chair in the kitchen, "Can I get you some water? Have you eaten anything?"

"Yes, thank you. I'm not hungry, and now that the war has ended, we all need to be careful we don't take too much."

"The war?" Eugene gave a puzzled look.

"Huh?" Lem struggled to recall the last words he said and blinked his way into the present. "Did I say something stupid? Not out of character, really, is it?" He smiled, that smile that no one could truly interpret.

"Just take a moment, have a seat," Eugene said with genuine empathy.

"A moment, yes." Lem said lowering himself to the chair with a sigh.

Eugene was sure Lem wasn't himself. What had he done? Everything he had worked for was just a disaster. Any doubts he had about his testing were now amplified, and he could hear the world laughing at him.

"We should leave the session today, Lem. You need some rest. Let me organise an Uber to take you home."

"Yes, home Mollie."

Eugene placed his hand on Lem's shoulder. "Just sit there a while. I am just going to cancel some other appointments so I can make sure you are OK."

Eugene made his way to the door and entered the lift to go up to his private floor.

"There are no other appointments today, Eugene." Daaisi interrupted.

"I know," Eugene replied tersely.

Daaisi's response tree implored silence, but the morality index had detected this to be extremely anomalous behaviour.

"Is the intention to assist Lem? Your schedule is clear today, except for the appointment with him."

"I know." Eugene was struggling to maintain his calm. "Don't let him leave the ground-floor interview room area." He used a very strict tone to imply an order, but Daaisi had no need for tone, the words were sufficient.

"Use your conversational application with him, particularly current events." Eugene wasn't sure what to do but also needed Daaisi out of his hair. "Don't let him sleep." Without thinking, he added "I will return to make him some coffee soon."

"Yes Eugene." Daaisi's calm vocalisation helped, but he needed some space.

Eugene entered his private office, taking a moment in his chair. He needed to take stock to be able to help.

Sometimes he found that was the best strategy.

Back up a bit and think.

***

If an artificial intelligence equipped with a care module has observed extreme short-term changes in the physical attributes of a target subject, can that be termed as worry?

If there was such a thing, Daaisi was worried.

Eugene's core physical readings were dangerously high. Higher than previously recorded. His sensory stimuli were hugely overactive, and his breathing was short. As equipped as an artificial intelligence may be, Daaisi was not equipped to triage serious medical issues, but it was clear Eugene was not to be disturbed by Daaisi's concerns for his own welfare.

As requested Daaisi began the conversation with Lem asking, "Did you arrive on your usual route via Centraal Station today, Lem?"

"Who me?" Lem was at first a bit confused and then remembered the bakery lady with her calm voice.

"No, dear," he said. "I think I walked. My feet certainly hurt."

Daaisi wasn't sure how to assist with sore feet. Most of the solutions seemed to be preventative.

As per Eugene's last instruction, Daaisi turned to current events. First on the conversational list of current events was always the weather, so Daaisi posed a question to Lem.

"How was the weather outside Lem?"

"It was raining quite heavily." Lem responded quickly.

Daaisi had weather reports of a clear but cold day, but the conversational module had conflict avoidance sub-routines, so Daaisi added a standard reply for poor weather and moved on.

"Rain does make it uncomfortable. Did you see that the Netherlands football team defeated Brazil in a friendly last night."

Lem rambled an answer about football being a game of haircuts these days and that results were fixed by dark, sinister gambling interests. Daaisi stored the answer, unsure of how to respond or even what a large part of the answer meant. Clearly, Lem had strong opinions and wasn't interested in the result or the score.

The next most popular news item was about mental health support for soldiers who have been on active service for the EU, UN, or NATO. Daaisi structured the question carefully to give neither a negative nor a positive slant to the question.

"Did you notice the Dutch government has given approval to the EU bill to provide mental health support to returning soldiers on EU, NATO, or even UN active service, including peacekeeping?"

Lem looked into the air.

"Did they!" He exclaimed, "about time."

"How could we send soldiers to war and not support them in every way on their return? They are putting their lives in jeopardy for us, and we abandon them, discarding them as used once they return. It's a tragedy. The government can waste money on so many things to please special interests, but it cannot find money for the care of those that protect our way of life. If you can't afford to care for the human in the soldier, don't send a man to war.

Daaisi's lightning-fast action on the conversational tree was a little unsure which part of the response should get the priority in any reply. Soldiers had a low percentage chance of death in peacekeeping, and Dutch soldiers had an even lower percentage in conflict. Mental health was increasingly affecting over eighty percent of returning veterans, but overwhelmingly, there was a one hundred percent chance that both men and women were participating in conflict, so Daaisi responded.

"Women also go to war."

Lem stopped, and without a target to aim, his vision focused on the ceiling.

"Stupid idea. Women should stay at home. We need that beauty to remain intact and not be sullied by the horror that rich, uninterested men produce for their greed."

"The change to women in front-line positions was made by many countries in the nineteen nineties." Daaisi replied.

Lem appeared perplexed.

"Nineties, you say?" His voice trailed off, and he sat staring into nowhere.

The use of 'you' as a pronoun or a determiner followed by the verb 'say' as a recital was very definitely the end of the conversation for Daaisi. Ensuring that further conversation would not be necessary, Daaisi also observed that Eugene was on the move and headed back to the kitchen.

***

Eugene entered the room finding Lem pondering something and asked the rhetorical question, "coffee Lem?"

"Oh, yes." Lem replied. It seemed whatever plane or time Lem was inhabiting, the offer of coffee was a universal godsend.

Eugene took his place behind the machine. Lem was still a little shaky about where or when he was. "Your bakery girl has some very modern ideas, Eugene."

"Really?" Eugene responded.

"Yes." Lem took on a higher pitch, like he was conveying gossip. "She said that women had been fighting on the front lines since the eighteen nineties. I find that a little hard to believe."

Eugene took a mental note to review the conversation later.

"The module for general conversation is new and needs some work." Eugene decided not to antagonise Lem, he wasn't really up for an argument himself. "The AI was just trying to use current news and events to engage you and perhaps structure questions to gauge your opinions."

Lem wasn't sure where to look now and felt any focus on Eugene might be aggressive, so he shrugged and breathed deeply to take in the smell of freshly ground coffee beans.

"Beautiful." his smile stretched across his face this time, leaving little doubt on the joy he felt.

Eugene felt affirmed that coffee was the saviour of the soul and the mediator of all conflicts. All he needed was for more world leaders to understand. His mind raced to a moment picturing Putin calmly sipping on a Raf coffee and listening to Erdogan extol the virtues of Turkish coffee while Xi made instant coffee grown in Vietnam and rubbed his hands quietly, happy with the profits.

Following his usual process, Eugene created an ambrosial cup with an extra-special swan with a rose above its head.

Lem looked wide-eyed as Eugene slid the cup over the bench.

"That's spectacular."

"Thanks Lem." Eugene took a moment, a breath and instantly felt better.

Following any kind of process could have been described as the great distiller of anxiety. He knew he just needed to be busy to bring himself back to earth.

The conversation between the two was light, but as time passed and coffee was consumed, Lem seemed to return to a more stable state of mind. His attention returned to the present, and his eclectic humour blended with his cantankerous demeanour made Eugene feel he was ready to head home.

Eugene arranged Lem an Uber and took him to the door as the vehicle arrived.

"I will get Daaisi to contact you regarding the next appointment Lem." Eugene didn't want to give up, but it was clear Lem needed time. "You take some time to relax, get some exercise, and don't sleep too much." Eugene smiled, and Lem smiled back, nodding knowingly.

***

Joost liked to walk through the park.

It was empty most days as winter set in, and more and more people were confined to their houses. Was it human contact they were avoiding? Conflict? Danger? Maybe it was just the weather?

Today had been a beautiful azure day, not freezing by Rotterdam standards but cold enough that his nostrils tingled and his breath clouded as he breathed out.

The park was littered with evidence of human interaction. Bottles of beer, leftover fast food containers. Obviously, the council workers had not visited yet, maybe it was the cold or just the general apathy that council work seemed to bring out in people.

Joost scanned the park, and for the first time in a long time, he noticed Lem sitting on one of the benches at the far end. Joost hadn't seen Lem since Mollie had passed. He had dropped in a few times but found Lem not at home, so he hadn't worried too much. He had spoken to Michael, who had said he was just busy and went out a lot, but seemed to be doing fine.

The path Joost took brought him close to where Lem was seated, As Joost got closer, he waved to Lem, hoping to catch his eye.

Lem seemed to not notice, or was just ignoring Joost.

"Lovely day," Joost said as he passed.

"Daisy said I should get some exercise. I wasn't going to come out here as she said it was going to rain, but it is perfect." Lem chuckled to himself. "AI is not so smart."

Some birds began to argue over some food left on the grass in front of them.

Joost decided it might be best to walk on.

***

"The next appointment with subject 259 is confirmed." Daaisi's message had arrived as instructed so as not to interrupt while he was playing music.

Daaisi had observed that message-based interruptions had a fifty three percent lower impact on Eugene's blood pressure than vocal messages when he was relaxing so had requested the modification, which Eugene had approved.

Debussy's Arabesque Number One Andantino con moto was so flowing, gentle, and relaxing, and its effect on his physical well-being was astounding.

Eugene had been going around in circles looking for storage, transport, or logic errors in Daaisi's development. After three days of looking, Eugene wasn't able to find any problems. So, given the lack of evidence to the contrary, he had to conclude that Lem knew Paige's boy. Whoever Lem was and whoever Paige's boy was. His anxious brain went into overdrive with possibilities, but his logical conclusions were that he just needed more evidence. He had lots of evidence from Paige, so he just needed more time with Lem, and Lem needed rest for that to continue.

He didn't respond to Daaisi, but the message continued.

"Inquiries regarding his health were positive. The appointment is secure for tomorrow."

"Please send an Uber to pick him up," Eugene said out loud. "I need him to arrive in one piece, relaxed, and on time, which would be nice."

"Yes, Eugene." Daaisi blended the vocalisation of the text into the music, not wanting to interrupt the effect it was having on Eugene, but following his previous instruction that you should respond using the communication mechanism you were first contacted with.

***

Lem was still late.

The Uber driver had arrived on time and sent numerous messages to Daaisi, who had sent them on to Lem, which he had duly ignored. The Uber driver had rung Lem's bell with no response and then called Daaisi, who had asked for some patience.

Uber in Rotterdam would give you ten minutes wait time. After that time had passed, as the driver went to drive away, he saw Lem in his rear view, waving frantically.

So Lem was late, but within normal parameters.

He sat down on the day bed in the interview room with a sigh. "Thanks for sending a car, Daisy. I know it was you." He smiled and winked.

Silence seemed the appropriate response, especially as Daaisi was unable to respond with a like-minded physical gesture.

"We have a new set of stimuli. Images and sounds that match the time period and give additional focus on textual detail." Daaisi announced, her voice melting over the airwaves. "Please relax."

Lem had already relaxed. His focus drifted as the images swirled. A mailbox, a bank, some advertising, a fancy tea cup, a cigarette packet, a fob watch, a ladies hairbrush, a street sign, a bottle opener, a coin, a glove, a hat, a cash register, a newspaper headline, a calendar. The images blurred as Lem's eyes closed.

Ragtime music played, with street sounds blended in, a crank start, a mouth organ, a backfire, and a shoe shine slowly trailing into silence.

***

Lem jolted awake. "Mollie," he cried.

The lights slowly illuminated, and Lem blinked with disbelief at his surroundings. "What!" he exclaimed.

"Where did she go?" Tears welling in his eyes. "Don't leave me."

"Your session is complete." Daaisi let the words drift in the air. Lem's responses were often difficult for Daaisi to interpret, but if AI could show interest, Daaisi was interested.

Lem sat silently, fighting back his tears.

Daaisi waited a further few minutes. One might think this would feel like an eternity for an artificial intelligence, but the three-hundred-and-sixty-six-second time cycles were no more or less strenuous than if it had been sixty or seven hundred and eighty thousand.

"When you are ready, coffee is being prepared in the kitchen."

Lem remained sitting silently, his shoulders drooping slightly. Finally, he raised his body dejectedly and made his way to the door.

In the kitchen, Eugene was focused on making coffee. He was lengthening the milk when Lem shuffled in.

"Everything OK, Lem?" he inquired.

Lem shrugged. "She had been right there. So real."

"They seem that way, don't they?" Eugene concurred. He had his own dreams that he would swear were reality, the people in them were close enough to touch. But they were dreams, maps of the past, search lights for the future, magnifications of the present.

"Daaisi had been working on some render improvements, so hopefully we would see the render in about ten more minutes."

"Estimated render time is seven minutes."

Eugene pointed to the roof. "As expected," he smiled at Lem, who seemed to be unaffected by the imminent coffee.

"Had anything been different this time?" Eugene quizzed excitedly.

"I was in the alley looking into the street today. I had never seen it from there before. The newspaper stand was in the centre."

Eugene smiled. The stimuli he had provided were designed to make that move. He had made those slight moves a science, but Lem made it easy.

"Mollie was being so sweet. There was Ragtime music playing, and she was dancing in the street." His face brightened for a moment, and then relapsed back to the point where he had just lost everything.

Eugene's smile evaporated. He had been silently congratulating himself, but with the cost of his success presented in front of him, the celebration had no taste.

"Render image is being displayed." Daaisi had broken the uncomfortable silence with an unexpected jolt.

The image was indeed from another angle on the street.

Mollie was dancing, the newspaper stand in full view, with three musicians playing in the background. Eugene could see the street sign in view. The name was clear as a beacon.

Everything he was never able to get from his own dreams was there in front of him.

Chapter Twelve

The future becomes as the past once was

"Lem has arrived at his residence." Daaisi announced.

"Let him rest for a few days. We have so much more information from the last render that we have a lot to do." Eugene said.

The render so clearly showed two key pieces of information. The street name is "Sixth Avenue." The drug store is "Bigelow Building."

"The Bigelow Building is a seven storey Romanesque-revival office building completed in nineteen hundred and two on sixth Avenue in New York City." Daaisi vocalised having already found the location. "The building was designed by John E. Nitchie for Clarence Bigelow's chemist business. It is still in existence today, and the Bigelow Pharmacy still runs out of the building."

"Is there any link to Lem?" Eugene enquired.

"Nothing I can determine. The pharmacy has been run by the Ginsberg family for two centuries."

Daaisi's voice was calm and clear.

"I've checked all connections to that family name across our previous searches and found nothing linking them to Lem."

"What about Mollie?"

"Also nothing." Daaisi replied.

Eugene checked the record of everything that had been searched, all were accessible, historical records in America.

A lot of the older records were kept in the National Archives, which Eugene had quietly compromised previously, so access was easy. Other records were in the Department of Health and State Department, which were difficult to access live, but Daaisi had dark web copies that covered the time frame they were looking for.

Mollie still remained a bit of a mystery.

Nothing of value existed in any Dutch government system. Mollie had obtained citizenship in the nineteen fifties, taking up residence after the Second World War. Her birth date was listed as nineteen eleven, that would make her over one hundred. Could she have been that old? Lem was only forty seven.

The age difference could have them as Aunt and Nephew. His parents, as listed on his birth certificate, who were much younger, died in a car accident when he was still a baby, and she took on sole responsibility. She is listed as a friend of the family, not a blood relative but it seemed no blood relative was willing to take on the responsibility.

Taxes and other documents showed nothing remarkable.

Eugene had spent over an hour inspecting the render, he even tried listening to Dark Side of the Moon, hoping the intricate depths of the music could evoke something special.

But to no avail.

"Break the render into four pieces and place each on the four large monitors in the viewing room." Eugene was grasping, but it was worth a try. "We might be missing something."

"Play, Led Zeppelin two, loud."

"Playing Led Zeppelin two in the viewing room."

Eugene walked into the viewing room as Robert Plant joined Jimmy Page and John Paul Jones, screeching his sexually charged lyrics over their thumping guitars. Eugene stood back from the four monitors to better take in the whole vista. The street image was not remarkable. It was any street in the USA, any time. Mollie's face shone as she danced to the music that must have been playing.

John Bonham crashed into the song as Eugene stood back and got some focus on the first screen.

The Bigelow Building was an interesting piece from the time.

"Display the Bigelow Building from the most recent source on monitor two."

It looked more or less the same, the signage had changed, but the cornice was still intact, paying homage to its history in a world that had little sympathy for such things.

"Revert to the previous enhanced render." Eugene gave precise instructions, even though Daaisi recognised his intention in the short version. It was a habit he was in. Habits are hard to break.

"Can you look up a list of all the deaths occurring in the Bigelow Building in the nineteen thirties?"

Eugene was guessing.

He had been messing with Lem's focus a lot, so the building may just be background noise.

"I have placed the list on monitor two," Daaisi advised.

Scanning the list, Eugene couldn't see anything relevant. Two decades of deaths were a lot to go through in New York in the lead-up to World War II.

"Store this list for future comparison." Eugene said. There was no doubt he was grasping at straws.

The second screen showed the bank. National City Bank of New York, there was nothing to see there. The tenant had been changed to a number of other stores since, and the owner had been a corporation since the turn of the nineteenth century.

"Do we have any employee records?" Eugene said, almost thinking out loud. "...or tax returns showing who employed Mollie at that time?"

The length of time it took Daaisi to respond let Eugene know the answer was not going to be easy.

He took the time to investigate the third screen showing the news stand. Lem's perspective was from the side, so there was not a lot of information to be gained.

The final screen showed the musicians setup in front of a bank that was closed. The musicians were African Americans, playing saxophone, drums, and double bass. They were captured performing, mojo in full flight, lost to the rhythm.

Lem said it was ragtime, which would fit the era.

Amazing detail for a first render.

Eugene saw nothing to give him the information he was looking for.

Frustrating.

The music in the viewing room played on... 'The Lemon Song', 'Heartbreaker', 'Ramble On'... Eugene tried to let the power of the music wash him over the line, but when the harmonica of 'Bring It on Home' wailed into the room, he knew that the image would yield no secrets by osmosis.

Maybe a coffee and a walk.

"I'll be out," he said to the air, trusting Daaisi would hear and process it.

The street was cold, but Eugene was well dressed, and the weather was perfect for walking. Rotterdam's usual blasting wind had died to a gentle breeze, and the sky was a brilliant crystal blue.

A walk would clear his mind, and he turned in the direction of his local coffee shop.

He had his usual espresso and tipped the waiter appropriately before making his way back to the dream bakery.

Eugene wasn't a paranoid man, but halfway up Oostzeedijk, a chill crept over him. A feeling he was being followed.

He stopped.

Behind him, the footsteps halted too.

He turned left away from the Dream Bakery, and the person followed him. He stopped in front of the tattoo parlour at the end of the street and looked into the reflection as the person took out some keys and opened the door to a house on the left.

"Paranoid," he thought.

Eugene backtracked and pushed open the door to the dream bakery as the lock clicked. He stared at himself in the door.

"Reflections," he thought.

He quickly made his way back to the viewing room and scanned all the images for reflections.

Eugene could see the reflection in the window of the bank. It showed the back of one of the musicians hats. The Panama hat had nothing visible from the front, but the render had placed a decorative feather in the back, which was only visible from the reflection.

He took a moment to wonder about the usually irrelevant detail the human brain stores from dreams.

There must be others.

"Focus on the panama hat of the saxophonist."

"Yes, Eugene." The second screen focused on the hat.

"Widen the shot to show the reflection of the hat in the bank window".

"Yes, Eugene." Now the hat and the feather could clearly be seen.

"Note the reflection, unlocking detail not available from the front in perspective."

"Yes, Eugene."

"Do we have another reflection you can determine in this or other renders?"

Eugene wasn't confident that Daaisi would know the difference between a reflection and another piece of detail. The render programme was complicated enough without adding reflective interpretation.

He scanned the image himself again.

"Zoom in on the news stand."

"Yes, Eugene." Screen one was focused more on the stand itself. It was sideways, with the attendants back showing. It looked like the attendant was checking his hair in a mirror. But you couldn't see the attendant. "Zoom in on the mirror in the news stand."

"Yes Eugene."

The image was of a newspaper hanging from the stand. The writing was reversed, but Eugene thought it said 'the world.'

"Increase focus." Eugene was short and to the point.

"Sorry, Eugene, the detail is at its maximum for the render."

"Okay. Show me an Internet-searched edition of 'The World' newspaper from New York."

The picture that came to the screen showed that it was the same newspaper. From the search picture, Eugene could see that the date was right underneath the logo.

He just needed better focus.

"Is there a way to increase focus in the render or re-render, giving particular insight into the details of this area?"

What felt like an eternity passed, Daaisi's words melted into the tension, inhibiting Eugene's breathing.

"That render will take thirty seven hours."

Eugene exhaled, dejected, but resolved.

"Let's get it started. Give this maximum priority."

***

"Seventh of July nineteen thirty four."

Daaisi's re-render was perfect. All the work done with Lem had given Daaisi access to his brain patterns for numbers, text, and a myriad of other details. Reflecting that detail was a simple module Daaisi had developed following Eugene's explanation and example.

Eugene had spent the time anxiously trying to distract himself. He resorted to music, movies, and first-person shooter games. He walked, he hummed, and he stressed. By the time the date came out, he was a mess of nerves.

"So what does that tell us?" The rhetorical question left Daaisi running a few wasted cycles before he interjected, "That was a rhetorical question. You should start a list of those."

"Yes Eugene. I have started the rhetorical question list and added it to my speech recognition module for future reference."

Daaisi continued, "there is nothing significant on that date in Greenwich Village listed in the archives. There were some speeches by Calvin Coolidge, the thirtieth US President. A baseball player called George Herman Ruth seemed to dominate the headlines. There is nothing specific to Mollie, the Ginsberg family or anything else of interest to our search."

"Let's scan around that date. Provide me a list of everything newsworthy a week on either side of that date."

"That search will take around fourteen hours, Eugene." The archive had a very slow search algorithm, and there was too much data to mirror.

"It is what it is?" Eugene resigned himself to more first-person shooter time.

***

"Okay." Eugene sighed.

"Nothing for one week, nothing for two weeks. Let's change this and only go forward for a further two weeks and see what we find."

Every other time he had changed Lem's perspective, the timeline had shifted, but only forward, never back. He had spent more time looking back through Lem's other renders, trying to work out more detail, looking for reflections or other points he may have missed but he didn't find anything significant. The news stand never had an angle like that, and any documents in and around the shoe shine or the drug stores showed nothing significant.

"I have a possible match, Eugene." Daaisi's words were auditory nectar.

"Maurice Third was killed in Greenwich Village on Greenwich Ave. on August seventh, nineteen thirty four. I am searching the archives for a photograph now."

The monitor flicked to a very old photograph, which, apart from the clothes and haircut of the time, was Lem. Same face, but with a very different expression. A wizened, knowledgeable, and almost powerful expression.

"That's Lem," Eugene gasped. "Maurice Third is Lem Forth?"

Eugene was now even more confused. "Is he related to Lem or Mollie?"

A dawning spread over Eugene's face.

"Or is it third to fourth? Is there something here?"

Eugene became a little lost in his own thoughts momentarily.

"Do we have a second and a first? Is this like a reincarnation?" his words sounded like complete nonsense.

He sat back and breathed out hard. Not a sigh, but more of a compressed release. This was not what he expected to find when he started this.

He pondered what to do next and confirmed with himself that he needed to get Lem back. He would keep this information to himself and focus on trying to get some more detail.

Eugene looked at the collage of images he had rendered from Lem's sessions. So, how does Paige's boy fit into all this? Maybe that should be his next stimulus.

Get a full look at the family and focus on the boy.

***

Process was important to Eugene.

Even though he really wanted to get Lem in fast, he let process happen and got Daaisi to arrange an appointment with Lem. The appointments were always scheduled via email, and so this one also needed to be.

Lem took a few days to answer the email but agreed to be ready for pickup. Eugene thought it best to send an Uber, and this time the pickup went smoothly. Lem seemed a little more switched on than the last appointment, still spacey but comprehensible.

"Lem's physical status has degraded by forty five percent since his first visit, and his mental state is visibly poor." Daaisi's advice wasn't needed, as Eugene could see this clearly.

It took Lem three tries to find the correct door when entering, but it had been his twenty-fifth visit to the dream bakery. Previously he had almost knocked down the interview room door trying to get started.

Eugene had instructed Daaisi to restart the consent application to regain Lem's consent prior to starting. He didn't need it as he already had it on file, but he also thought it couldn't hurt. The consent protocol used the phrase, "you can cease this test at any time by uttering the word 'cease'. Do you understand?"

Lem had paused like he was playing musical chairs and had to decide which chair to go for based on who else was standing around him, relevant to the chair placement.

Eugene almost bit his tongue when Lem uttered words in the affirmative.

The stimulus package was very tailored. Possibly Eugene's most tailored package ever. The package included pictures of the boy that Daaisi had allowed from Paige's renders blended with the street, pictures of the drug store and bank, and images he had found from a search on 'The World' newspaper. The music he used was city street sounds and a compilation of ragtime songs. Maple Leaf Rag, Elite Syncopation, and The Entertainer by Scott Joplin, followed by Black and

White by George Botsford. Eugene had never used music before but it seemed to fit.

According to his brain patterns, Lem never got to relish the energy of black and white as sleep came to claim his consciousness quickly. When Daaisi had asked earlier after his welfare, Lem couldn't really recall his sleep patterns, so maybe he hadn't slept for a while. Eugene watched as Lem's brain melted into REM sleep, and the activity went dark for a while. He didn't usually watch subjects in this state, but this detail was going to answer so many of his own personal questions that he wanted to see and understand. Lem twitched slightly, adjusting his body to meet his mind. The time seemed to pass slowly for Eugene, and he busied himself with part of a new security module for Daaisi.

"Lem's vitals show some alarming trends, Eugene." Daaisi interrupted his thoughts, which had been lost in code for an hour.

"Vitals on my screen." Eugene internally chastised himself for getting distracted. "Details from the last hour."

The information in front of him showed Lem's degradation since his mind and body first greeted sleep an hour ago. His dream had just started, and his body seemed to be struggling to keep up the pace.

"Wake him up." Eugene said to Daaisi. "Turn on the lights and play the exit music."

"Yes Eugene."

Lem's vitals dropped to zero.

"Is that malfunctioning?" Eugene implored, almost pleadingly.

"No, Eugene, Lem Forth's heart has stopped."

Eugene immediately rushed to the lift on the first floor. By the time he arrived at Lem's side and took his pulse, there was nothing.

Eugene had minimal medical equipment in the building and certainly had no defibrillation equipment.

"Hospital." Eugene thought, "I should get him to a hospital."

There were several hospitals in the area. But then there would be questions.

"Daaisi, I have no pulse. Is he deceased?" Eugene already knew the answer.

"Is this a rhetorical question, Eugene?" Daaisi replied.

"No," Eugene bit back.

"Yes, Eugene. Lem Forth has no pulse and no brain activity, which are both definitions of deceased."

Eugene sighed. Not being a sigh of relief, but the kind where you know there is trouble to come and you are in the midst of it. He sat for a few minutes, holding Lem's wrist, hoping a pulse might return. His thoughts skipped through scenarios, flirting with possibilities.

He narrowed it down to a single decision.

"Should I call the emergency services?" Daaisi inquired with a calmness and emotional detachment.

Eugene thought through the scenario. The ambulance would come, there was nothing to be done as Lem was dead. The police would come and ask questions. Difficult questions. He could hear them now.

Research?

With modified medical equipment? What type of experiments? Do you have a license? We will need to collect all the information and look through the evidence.

His whole life would be laid bare, and his research would stop. Five years of his life wasted, and if he is found culpable in any way, maybe another five or ten.

He let go of Lem's hand and went to the cupboard in the interview room to get a blanket. He gently removed the dream interceptor from Lem's head, set his body straight on the bed, and laid the blanket over him."

Eugene moved to the kitchen and took a bottle of whisky from the top cupboard. Eugene wasn't a big drinker, but he enjoyed particularly good Irish whisky. His collection was extensive, including several Jameson's variations, Tullamore Dew, and Bushmills, but on this occasion he went for a West Cork single malt.

Eugene savoured the well-balanced palate, allowing the dried apple and honey to wash over his jowls, bracing for the baking-spice finish. The moment gave him time to think and time to consider. Another sip and a plan came to mind.

"Daaisi, is there a park near Lem's apartment? Put the map on the screen in the kitchen."

"Yes Eugene. From my conversations with Lem, he visits this park regularly."

"Lem had no known relatives or associates, friends, acquaintances, or anything, correct?" Again, this could have been counted as a rhetorical question, as Eugene knew the answer.

"No known associates, friends, or acquaintances, and no living relatives." The answer was the confirmation Eugene needed.

Eugene looked up at the park. It had four paths leading in and out. One path in particular was from a back street, which he could easily access without being disturbed.

"Book me an Uber to Lem's apartment." Eugene called as he moved up the stairs again to his private floor.

Dressing himself in a peaked cap and a large coat, Eugene had a plan formulating. Just needed one more sip of whisky to give him the bravado he needed.

"Place the building in high security mode, no one in or out, advise me of any camera action by message while I am out. I will be taking the secure handset. Play the Lord of the Rings trilogy for me on my bedroom TV and change the temperature in the interview room to as cold as possible."

Eugene knew he had time.

***

Eugene said nothing in the Uber. He had dressed himself simply, as close to what Lem would wear as his wardrobe would allow. He threw a black hooded jacket over the rest of his outfit to ensure anonymity once he got out.

He didn't wave at the Uber driver on exit and moved along Lem's street towards the park silently. He surveyed the street for possible capture points, noticing a camera focused on the door and front window of the flower shop and a Council CCTV focused on the entry to the park.

He assessed the park CCTV, luck was on his side as it was focused on anti social behaviour coming from the local estate building with coverage around the exit Lem would be unlikely to use.

He kept his back to the camera and moved into the park looped around and saw a number of quiet park benches towards the back. He noticed the exit close by, no empty car parks but a quiet passage in and out none the less.

Eugene walked slowly through the exit and saw nothing of interest. A good boring Rotterdam street.

The whisky was beginning to wear off and the evening air was cold, brutally cold even for Rotterdam. He had already resolved to walk back to the Dream Bakery which should take him around thirty minutes. The walk took him forty five as he avoided public cameras and any private CCTV he might see.

To his surprise he received no alerts from Daaisi.

Why would he?

Just paranoid.

***

The conditions were right for it, but in no way was Eugene able to influence the weather. That night in Rotterdam, just after Eugene's very indistinct Lava Grey Audi pulled away from Sint-Jacobs Park, it snowed.

Lem was propped up on the park bench, still lost in his dream.

On his return, Eugene, with Daaisi's assistance, had compromised the public CCTV system and looked at the footage from the afternoon and from his time in the park, including footage possibly of Lem being placed on the bench. Since nothing appeared incriminating, he left the footage intact.

He kept the footage on his own CCTV showing Lem arriving and edited the footage from the previous week to show Lem leaving.

Lucky for him, Lem had limited fashion options and was regularly wearing the same clothes.

In those few sips of whisky, Eugene had decided to hide in plain sight. He made plans to start subtle preparations, to move quickly if he had to. Too much would be suspicious. He fully expected to be contacted by police as the Dream Bakery would be Lem's last stop before he died, but hopefully the park would create enough distance, if not absolve him of blame, lacking the evidence to outright accuse him.

Eugene had a story ready.

Lem had been helping him with some marketing research. He would cooperate, hand over the details, and provide lists of others who had participated. He even got Daaisi to book more test subjects quickly, to muddy the evidence around the interview room and make it look like it was business as usual. Finally, he would send a request for another appointment to Lem in a few days.

"Render is complete on Lem's final session." Daaisi announced unexpectedly. With all his other activities, Eugene didn't even realise that there was enough data to allow a complete render.

"Kitchen Screen," Eugene barked.

It was late but another whisky would help him sleep if such a thing was possible.

The picture was up on the screen when he walked into the kitchen.

It was a familiar scene, the street, the drugstore, and the bank. But in this picture, the father had wrapped his body around the boy and his wife.

The boy's head was glaring out from underneath his father's jacket, eyes fixed on a large man in a trench coat holding a Thompson *M1921A* machine gun pointed directly at Lem, or Maurice.

Maurice held up his hand, defiantly willing the bullets away from Mollie with his will. Mollie was like a stone cowering behind him holding tightly in her hand a half heart fob.

Eugene dropped his eyes.

Lem had died in his dream.

Eugene had known they were on the path to something sinister, but he never imagined this.

Yet, here they were.

He still had so much to learn and so far to go, but now he was convinced this had been a past life. The physical evidence he had uncovered matched the rendered dream images with astonishing detail, even though they seemed to raise more questions than they answered.

Mollie, Lem, and Maurice had a link, and Mollie seemed to know about it. Maybe Maurice knew about it as well. Some ability they had discovered to be able to trace each others appearance next in the circle of life, maybe something like the Tibetan monks in the eternal search for the Dalai Lama. But Eugene had never read anything about normal people doing that.

How was this possible?

It appeared something Lem didn't have or Mollie didn't teach him.

Eugene swirled the whisky in the glass breathing deeply over the rich liquid before taking a prelusive nip.

The whisky failed to warm the cold that gripped him.

Had he just uncovered that connection?

What did he do with it now?